P9-BYF-992

Babe in
BOYLAND

Jody Gehrman

Babe in BOYLAND

Dial Books

an imprint of Penguin Group (USA) Inc.

DIAL BOOKS
An imprint of Penguin Group (USA) Inc.
Published by The Penguin Group
Penguin Group (USA) Inc., 375 Hudson Street, New York, NY 10014, U.S.A.

Penguin Group (Canada), 90 Eglinton Avenue East, Suite 700, Toronto, Ontario, Canada M4P 2Y3 (a division of Pearson Penguin Canada Inc.) • Penguin Books Ltd, 80 Strand, London WC2R 0RL, England • Penguin Ireland, 25 St. Stephen's Green, Dublin 2, Ireland (a division of Penguin Books Ltd) • Penguin Group (Australia), 250 Camberwell Road, Camberwell, Victoria 3124, Australia (a division of Pearson Australia Group Pty Ltd) • Penguin Books India Pvt Ltd, 11 Community Centre, Panchsheel Park, New Delhi - 110 017, India • Penguin Group (NZ), 67 Apollo Drive, Rosedale, North Shore 0632, New Zealand (a division of Pearson New Zealand Ltd) • Penguin Books (South Africa) (Pty) Ltd, 24 Sturdee Avenue, Rosebank, Johannesburg 2196, South Africa • Penguin Books Ltd, Registered Offices: 80 Strand, London WC2R 0RL, England

Designed by Nancy R. Leo-Kelly
Text set in ITC Esprit
Printed in the U.S.A.
5 7 9 10 8 6 4

Library of Congress Cataloging-in-Publication Data
Gehrman, Jody Elizabeth.
Babe in boyland / by Jody Gehrman.
p.   cm.
Summary: Natalie, a seventeen-year-old former drama club member who now writes a relationship column for her school newspaper, decides to go undercover as a student at an all-boys boarding school so that she can figure out what guys are really like.
ISBN 978-0-8037-3274-2 (hardcover)
[1. Sex role—Fiction. 2. Interpersonal relations—Fiction. 3. Boarding schools—Fiction. 4. Schools—Fiction. 5. Theater—Fiction.] I. Title.
PZ7.G25937Bab 2011   [Fic]—dc22   2010011876

For my editors,
Lauri Hornik and Liz Waniewski.
Lauri, thanks for trusting me with your baby;
Liz, thanks for seeing beyond the awkward,
angsty stages of early drafts.
You're both brilliant.

Babe in
BOYLAND

Chapter One

My name is Natalie Rowan. Everyone knows that. Only a select few, however, know I'm the evil genius behind my nom de plume, Dr. Aphrodite. That might seem like a pretty hefty title for a seventeen-year-old junior who's not even sure she's officially made it to what my mom refers to as "heavy petting." (Ew. I know. But my other option's "third base," which is suspiciously '80s, right? Come on, inventors-of-sexual-euphemisms, get on the job!)

To be honest, I dig having a secret identity, even if it is kind of a misnomer. I think everyone should have at least a part of them that's self-invented; in fact, the world would be much more interesting if we all created our own identities afresh whenever we felt like it. Otherwise you're just walking around regurgitating what's expected, which is like, why bother? I actually plan to mess up my life and start over every seven years. That way, I'll never get in a rut. I read somewhere that most of your cells only live about seven years anyway, so in theory you literally *are* a new person; I figure that's the best time to start over.

I created Dr. Aphrodite when I started writing our school paper's relationship column last year. It's mostly a Dear Abby type deal, where people write in with questions about love or sex or whatever and I answer them. Occasionally I sound off blog-style on some current obsession of mine—as long as I can get it past our semi-fascist censors and it's relationship-oriented, you'll see it in my column. I've covered topics like Promnesia (when perfectly sane people forget about everything except spray tans, strapless dresses, and dyed-to-match pumps), Brazilaphobia (fear of overly zealous hair removal), and Face Relations (getting it on with people via Facebook).

Just so you know, being Dr. Aphrodite isn't always easy. I have to guard my clandestine writing life so carefully, I sometimes feel like a secret agent. I sort of hoped writing about romance might help me scare up a little of my own, but so far that plan hasn't worked in the slightest. While I dispense sage advice to the masses about how to make their love lives thrive, my own is virtually nonexistent. That's one of the reasons nobody can know my alias; who's going to seek advice from a love expert who's never been in love? Even though my column's super-popular, it doesn't exactly earn me friends and admirers. Only my two best friends and my editors know it's me behind the smoke and mirrors. You'd think at least they would respect me for my massive following, but I sometimes suspect they don't take Dr. Aphrodite very seriously.

Which is sad, really. Because what's more serious than love?

As I walk into the Journalism room, I can hear my editors, Rachel Webb and Chas Marshal, snickering. They're hunched over the computer screen, avidly reading something on the *Mountain View News* website. At the sound of my footsteps Rachel turns. For a second she looks caught, but the guilty impulse passes almost instantly from her face. Her eyes sparkle as she peers at me over her glasses, pink rabbit nose twitching with delight.

"Look at this one," Chas says, all excited. "Some guy actually called her a—"

Without taking her eyes off mine, Rachel lets out a polite little cough.

Chas spins around and, seeing me, plasters on a fake smile. "Hi, Natalie."

Rachel says, "How's Dr. Aphrodite?"

"Fine." My voice comes out high-pitched and nervous; my gaze flits from Rachel to Chas and back again. "What's up?"

"Your latest column's getting lots of attention." Chas leans back in his chair. "Have you seen the message board?"

"Not since last night. Why? What's going on?" My tongue suddenly feels dry as sandpaper.

He stands and gestures at his chair. "Go ahead—check it out. We haven't gotten this many comments since those hackers posted porn on our homepage."

Reluctantly, I sit. The page shows my column, its borders afflicted with hearts and cupids. I was able to override the cheesy layout in our print version, but somehow it slipped through online. Bleh. I write a thought-provoking, cutting-edge column about dating in the new millennium, not a Hallmark card. Whatever. I skim my column, comforted somewhat by its familiarity.

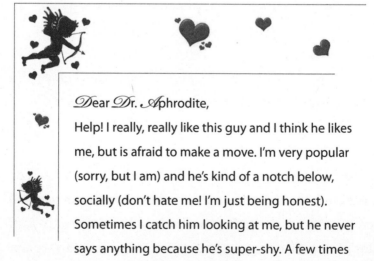

Dear Dr. Aphrodite,

Help! I really, really like this guy and I think he likes me, but is afraid to make a move. I'm very popular (sorry, but I am) and he's kind of a notch below, socially (don't hate me! I'm just being honest). Sometimes I catch him looking at me, but he never says anything because he's super-shy. A few times

I've tried to start up conversations with him, but it didn't go anywhere. I think he's intimidated by my social status. Should I ask him out?

Sincerely,

Hot for the Art Boy

Dear H-FAB,

I can see your quandary. You're a gorgeous, charismatic, goddess of fabulosity (I don't know you, but I'm reading between the lines). Art Boy is obviously intimidated! You're like the sun and he's squinting up at you, barely able to see because of your blinding radiance.

Should you ask him out? Of course you should! I bet he's pining away for you right this second, trying to work up the courage just to say hi. Put the boy out of his misery! What do you have to lose? If he says yes, and he can get over his inferiority complex, you might make a great couple. If he says no, don't even trip; it would only prove that he's too insecure to handle your tremendous power and beauty.

I scan the page and see a series of comments have been posted—fifty-three, to be exact. As I reach for the mouse and scroll down to view them, I can feel cold sweat breaking out along the back of my neck. Chas mutters something under his breath and Rachel suppresses a laugh, which turns into an unattractive snorting sound. I shoot her a dark look; she bites her lip.

Posted by: Shredder103

I've been reading your column ever since you started it last year, and I haven't said anything, but I've got to speak up because it's getting out of control. Every single week girls write to you for advice and all you ever tell them is what they want to hear. You have no idea how guys think or feel about anything! All you're doing is helping girls at this school perpetuate their delusions about the world and how it works. Not once have you ever told them anything useful or sane from a guy's point of view. Do us all a favor and stop!

Posted by: BeerHog

i fully agree w/ shredder. who do u think u r dr. aphrodite? last month my gf wrote u complaining i play video games when i should be w/ her and now she's nagging me about going 2 couples counseling. COUPLES COUNSELING? WTF??? im 15!!! damn, gimme a break.

Posted by: Joey

srsly, ur ruining our lives! all the chicks @ mt view high

listen to u and all u do is fill their heads w/ BS!! chas, fire her already!!!

Posted by: Duckmanrocks

Can anyone say "delusions of grandeur"? That's what happens when you lose touch with reality and start to believe your own hype. That's what happens to girls when they listen to you, Dr. Aphrodite. There are approximately nine hundred girls who go to school here, and as far as I can tell at least eight hundred ninety-seven of them have been poisoned by your column. My sister took your advice and gave her boyfriend an ultimatum: He had to stop playing Texas Hold'em with his friends every Thursday night or she'd dump him. Guess what? He didn't stop. So she dumped him. Now she's miserable, and her boyfriend's with some other chick, one of the three who doesn't read your column, apparently. You really think you helped my poor sister? She cries herself to sleep every night. I've got to wear earplugs. Thanks a lot.

Posted by: Moshi-moshi
Yeah, what he said!

Posted by: Joey

see, chas? every1 agrees! give her the ax!!

Posted by: ZombieKing

What does Dr. Aphrodite know about love or sex?

When's the last time she got any?

And so on. The abuse goes on and on. Every once in a while someone pipes up in my defense—always a girl and obviously one of my fans. I turn away from the computer when I can't take any more and fold my arms in front of my chest, forcing myself to look Chas in the eye.

"Any publicity's good publicity, right? At least they're reading. That's really something when you consider how illiterate most of these idiots are." It takes all my concentration to keep my voice from trembling. An ache behind my eyes tells me tears are imminent, but I refuse to give in. Not here. Not in front of these two, the editorial team from hell. I'm going to write a book someday called *The Devil Wears His-and-Her Gap Cardigans*. Everyone knows I should be in line for editor-in-chief next year, but Chas is obviously grooming Rachel for the position instead. Together, they're so condescending they make me feel like the literary equivalent of chewing gum—cheap, saccharine, and utterly disposable.

"That's a good attitude." Chas's smile shows no teeth.

10

"Actually, that's precisely the attitude readers are offended by," Rachel says.

"What's that supposed to mean?" I snarl.

"You're cocky, Natalie. You think all girls are superior to guys or something. It's reverse sexism." She cuts her eyes at Chas. "You've heard of misogyny? This is mansogyny!"

I groan in response. Ridiculous.

Chas hoists his laptop bag over his shoulder. "Well, I'm not going to fire you, so don't worry."

"Gee, thanks." Like he even could! There's nothing else in his pathetic rag readers bother with, and they both know it. The only reason they're gloating about this whole fiasco is because they're jealous of my column's popularity.

Chas pushes his glasses up onto the bridge of his nose. "Guess we'll catch you later. We're headed to the library."

"Yeah?" I feign interest, eager to change the subject. "What are you working on?"

"Story of the Year entries are due a week from Monday." Rachel's tone implies only serious drug users could possibly miss such an important deadline.

"What's that?"

She nods at the announcement board. It's meticulously arranged, with a border of yellow corrugated paper and shiny capital letters at the top saying MOUNTAIN VIEW NEWS. Under that is a typed notice that reads *Please consult with Assistant Editor Rachel Webb before posting your announcements.* Everything on it is perfectly straight, like she took a ruler and lined each notice up before impaling the edges with shiny silver thumbtacks. Rachel points at the Day-Glo yellow paper neatly tacked to the very center of the board. *Story of the Year Award,* it says. *Win $1,000. Show your potential as an investigative reporter by covering a social issue relevant to your generation. Deadline: Monday, September 20, 5:00.*

"Oh, yeah," I say. "I was thinking I should enter something."

After a moment of silence, Chas and Rachel burst out laughing.

"What's so funny?"

"You're hardly an investigative reporter, Natalie." Chas punches my arm lightly.

"So? I'm a writer. I know how to do research."

Rachel catches her breath and puts on a mock-serious face. "When they say 'a social issue relevant to your generation,' they're not talking about H-FAB and her crush on Art Boy."

This cracks them up. I glower.

"This just in!" Chas says in a cheesy reporter voice. "H-FAB and Art Boy Go to Homecoming!"

I offer the weakest of smiles. "What are you guys writing yours on?"

"Prescription drug abuse." Chas nods. "It's a real epidemic."

"Eating disorders," Rachel says solemnly. "Speaking of which, are any of your friends bulimic? I need a good quote."

"Sorry." I shrug. "No one I know enjoys puking."

"Don't get offended. It's common among theater types, and I know you used to act."

"None taken." Which isn't exactly a lie, since of all the things they've said to me in the past ten minutes, this is the least insulting.

"All right, see you," Chas says, heading for the exit. "Get to work on that H-FAB piece. Sounds like a front-page feature."

They're still laughing as they walk out the door.

When they're gone, I go back to the Day-Glo announcement and read it again. I try to picture the expressions Chas and Rachel will wear when they learn I've won. For once in their lives, they won't look so smug. They think Dr. Aphrodite's a big joke, huh? Think she can't investigate? They're about to realize just how serious Dr. Aphrodite can get.

●●●●●●●●●●●●●●●●●●
Chapter Two
●●●●●●●●●●●●●●●●●●

*A*s I'm driving away from campus, I get a text from Darcy that reads simply *My house. Now. Rob's a dick.* Between reading her text and thinking about that damn message board, I'm so distracted I almost drive up onto the sidewalk, where a startled blonde is walking her Pomeranian. Fantastic— just what I need to make my day complete: vehicular manslaughter plus first-degree dogicide.

At Darcy's house, I park the Buick haphazardly in the general vicinity of the curb, throw open the gate, and dash straight to Darcy's room, which has its own entrance. Her walls are completely covered with posters of Jim Morrison. She's got a thing for him, don't ask me why.

Darcy's a drama nerd, big-time. We've been in plays together since we were like seven. Up until the end of freshman year, I was way into theater too. That's when Summer Sheers moved up from LA and started stealing every single role from me, instantly demoting me from ingénue to understudy. It pissed me off so much that I stopped auditioning and started pouring my creative energy into a new role: Dr. Aphrodite. Now that's going downhill too. Great. I'm seventeen with two failed careers already.

"Darcy?!"

She appears in her bedroom doorway, eyes red from crying. "He blew me off again."

"No!"

"Yes!" she wails. "He was supposed to meet me after fifth period, but he never showed. I saw him drive off with Michiko Tanabe. Stupid prick!"

I pull her into my arms and she unleashes a torrent of hiccupping sobs. "Shh . . ."

"I saw Michiko wearing a Dave Matthews T-shirt the other day! Do you have any idea how much Rob hates Dave Matthews?"

"Sit down," I say, pulling her down onto the oversized beanbag at our feet. "Tell me everything."

"So you know we hooked up last weekend, right?"

I nod. Rob is Darcy's on-again-off-again messed-up angst-ridden mini-rocker boyfriend. He's like five foot three with a concave chest. Amazingly, the chicks dig him. He's in a band called PigHead. Going to their gigs makes me want to rupture my own eardrums with an ice pick.

"I know this sounds stupid after everything we've been

through . . ." she says, her throat thick with phlegm from all the crying, "but I seriously thought we were at a new level. He told me . . . he actually said . . ."

"Okay, hold on." I dig through my purse and produce a Kleenex.

She blows her nose violently a couple times, then resumes. "He said he could picture us in LA together."

I furrow my brow. "What, like you'd live there together after high school, you mean?"

"Well," she hedges, "he didn't exactly specify . . ."

I nod encouragement at her.

"But he plans on moving there after graduation, so what else could he mean, right? It seemed like . . . not a commitment, exactly, but a step in that direction . . ." She trails off.

"You're probably right," I say, trying to sound positive.

Suddenly the door flies open and Chloe saunters in, cell pressed to her ear. "Okay then, see you tomorrow? . . . No can do, rehearsal at six—how about four? . . . Perfect. Ciao!" She shoves the phone into her giant purse, then slumps into the dilapidated La-Z-Boy in the corner. "My emergency Darcy ringtone went off. Make it quick, though, I've got a mani-pedi in twenty minutes."

"Excuse me, Your Highness," I scold. "What's more important? Darcy's emotional health, or your nails?"

Chloe holds both hands out, examining them. "Can I think about that a minute?"

I look at them—my two best friends—and feel a pang of affection. They're about as different from each other as two people can possibly be. Darcy's short and curvy with a pierced tongue, hot pink hair, and a wicked sense of humor. She's the girl you'd want with you if you ever got stranded in some deadly Amazonian jungle; despite her current Rob-related meltdown, she's totally level-headed and possesses MacGyver-like ingenuity in a crisis, so long as it's someone else's. Chloe, in contrast, has long auburn hair, olive skin, designer everything, and a body to die for. Her sense of humor is an acquired taste, seeing as it's wry and a little sadistic, but her loyalty runs deep. The three of us have been best friends since the second grade, when we were cast together in *The Wizard of Oz*. Darcy was Glinda, Chloe was the Wicked Witch, and I was Dorothy; that right there speaks volumes about our dynamics.

Chloe rolls her eyes. "I'm kidding! Darcy's freak-out is way more important."

"Thank you." I turn back to Darcy. "Now, you were saying . . . ?"

"Although it would be nice if we could wrap this up in fifteen," Chloe adds, looking at her watch.

"Ignore her," I growl. "So, last weekend with Rob seemed promising, right?"

Darcy sniffles, wiping away tears with the back of her

hand. "Yeah! We went to his house after the gig, and he was really sweet and considerate—"

"Was he stoned?" Chloe interrupts.

Darcy avoids her eyes. "A little."

"Darcy!" Chloe leans forward, forcing Darcy to look at her. "How many times are you going to put yourself through this? He's all lovey-dovey when he's high, and then Monday he's an asshole! You can't base a relationship on his bong."

"Don't be so harsh!" I say to Chloe, wrapping an arm around Darcy's shoulder protectively.

Chloe crosses her arms and says to me, "Go on . . ."

"What?"

"Isn't this where you weave elaborate excuses for him?" Chloe imitates my voice. "'He's afraid of the passion he feels for you, Darcy! He can only love you openly when he's stoned because that's the only time he can deal with your bewitching power over him, blah blah blah.'"

I just stare at her, speechless. She's right. I do say that kind of stuff. All the time. It's my role—the optimistic, innocent Dorothy. I tell my friends what they want to hear: that they're amazing, and the guy they like is only frightened of his feelings, and they should just believe in themselves and hang in there and not let his insecurities get in the way. I think of all those comments from the message board today.

Who do you think you are, Dr. Aphrodite?

Can anyone say "delusions of grandeur"?

What does Dr. Aphrodite know about love or sex? When's the last time she got any?

"Um . . . Natalie?" Darcy looks worried. "What's wrong?"

I open my mouth to speak, but nothing comes out.

All the chicks at Mountain View High listen to you and all you do is fill their heads with BS!!!

Not once have you ever told them anything useful or sane from a guy's point of view.

You have no idea how guys think or feel about anything!

"Oh my God." I blink at Darcy and Chloe, feeling dazed. "They're totally right."

"Who's right?" Chloe squints at me, confused.

"All those guys who want me fired. I'm a complete fake."

Darcy shoots a look at Chloe. "What's she talking about?"

"I have no idea." Chloe snaps her fingers in front of my face. "Natalie? You with us? You hearing voices?"

I quickly fill them in on the whole message board fiasco. They make sympathetic noises, though Chloe surreptitiously glances at her watch.

"They're just threatened because you're on our side," Darcy says.

"Maybe that's the problem. I tell girls what they want to hear, but does that really help them? I have no idea how

guys see things." I stand up and start pacing. "Take your relationship with Rob, for example. How long have you been
with him?"

"On and off for about a year."

"And when he ditches you for some other girl, what happens?"

Darcy winces at my out-of-character bluntness, then
looks doubtful. "I call you . . . ?"

"Right! You call us, and Chloe makes some snide remark,
usually about Rob's lack of hygiene—"

"Because he seriously needs to wash his hair at least once
a week," Chloe says.

"And then I launch into a complicated analysis of his
modus operandi, always assuming that he adores you (because who wouldn't?) and he worships you (because he
should)." I stop pacing and look Darcy in the eye. "But
what if I'm wrong? What if he doesn't even like you that
much?"

Darcy's lower lip quivers slightly, but I press on.

"And all this time I've been encouraging you to give him
the benefit of the doubt, when really the situation is hopeless because he doesn't respect you and he's not going to
change."

A stunned silence. They both stare at me.

"The point is, who am I to give advice about love? I
haven't had a real boyfriend like . . . ever."

Chloe raises an eyebrow. "She seems to be having what they call an 'epiphany.'"

"You really think Rob doesn't like or respect me?" Darcy whispers.

"I don't have the slightest idea what Rob feels!" My voice rises with increasing urgency. "That's the problem! I'm a terrible advice columnist because I only understand half of the equation—the girl side. The other half is a complete mystery."

"I'm confused," Chloe says. "Is this Natalie's identity crisis, or Darcy's love crisis? Because I only have time for one or the other."

I collapse next to Darcy again on the beanbag. "I'm sorry. That was insensitive. You're sad about Rob and we should just, you know, focus on that."

To my surprise, Darcy doesn't look all that tearful anymore. "You know what? I'm sick of being sad about Rob."

"Thank God," Chloe says under her breath.

Darcy sits up straighter. "I think you're right, Natalie. I've made way too many excuses for him, and I'm sick of it."

"Amen," Chloe sighs.

"I was supposed to go to his gig tonight, but screw it! My parents are out of town all weekend. You know what we're going to do?" Darcy's eyes light up with mischief. "We're going to party!"

"Now you're talking," Chloe says.

Darcy jumps up and claps her hands. "Sound the alarms, girls. I'm officially single, starting now, and I feel a serious case of rebound coming on!"

Chloe pulls out her cell. "Okay, screw it. I'm canceling my appointment. If we're throwing a spontaneous rebound bash, you're going to need my help."

The two of them launch into preparations with serious verve; they blast music, text everyone we know, dig through the pantry in search of plastic cups. I try to get into the spirit of things for Darcy's sake, but I'm still reeling from the day's events. It's a little hard to concentrate on a party when my whole world is collapsing. How can I possibly keep Dr. Aphrodite alive now that I know what a phony she is? Maybe Rachel and Chas were right—maybe I am a total joke. Who do I think I am, posing as an expert in spite of my cluelessness about guys' hearts, brains, and other vital organs? All this time I've been telling Darcy and hundreds of others just like her exactly what they want to hear. It turns out I've been harming them, not helping. I've been reckless and irresponsible, handing out advice when I'm completely unqualified. Dr. Aphrodite is a quack! I feel all naked and exposed. Everyone else can see what a fool I was, what a sham; I'm the last to get it.

"Natalie, you okay?" Darcy notices me staring out the

window and puts a hand on my shoulder, interrupting my morbid shame spiral.

"Yeah. Just got a lot to think about, I guess."

"Don't be too hard on yourself." She squints at me, reading my mind. She's always been able to do that—see right through my shell, into my messy internal world. "Dr. Aphrodite kicks ass."

"You might be her only fan."

"Already your advice has helped me." She holds up a frosty glass. "Well, that and these mocha shakes Chloe made. You've got to try one."

"Okay, okay, twist my arm." I allow her to lead me into the kitchen, where Chloe's dancing, pouring espresso into the blender, and checking her messages all at the same time.

Yes, I might be a washed-up advice columnist, a failed love goddess, a journalistic joke. I do have a couple reasons to live, though: It's Friday and I've got caffeine-wielding friends.

It's not much, but it's something.

●●●●●●●●●●●●●●●●●●●●
Chapter Three
●●●●●●●●●●●●●●●●●●●●

I get the idea for my exposé in Darcy's parents' bathroom. The three of us are in there getting ready for the party. Darcy's applying canary yellow eye shadow and Chloe is trying out her new flatiron. I'm sitting on the edge of the tub painting my toenails a shiny candy apple red. Chloe's going on about this guy she met recently, Josh.

"He's gorgeous," she's saying. "Bright blue eyes, perfect skin, great body. Plus he smells so clean!"

Darcy laughs. "You're obsessed with hygiene."

"So? There are worse obsessions. I started carrying hand sanitizer, and I'm not above using it on others. Bacteria, germs, bodily fluids—ew! Such a turn-off."

Chloe's mom is a toxicologist; I think she may have gone a little overboard in teaching her daughter about the importance of cleanliness. Chloe once broke up with a guy because he stopped by her house after a run. She

24

said the smell of sweat lingered in her nasal cavities for days.

"Get over it," I tell her for the millionth time, "a little dirt is natural. You shouldn't be so phobic."

"I have standards! What can I say?" She pulls out her compact to examine how her hair looks in the back. "I just want to know how Josh really feels. I mean, he flirts with me, but what's that say? Doesn't mean he actually likes me. Guys are so hard to read."

Darcy scoffs. "Tell me about it. I would pay so much money just to know what Rob's thinking for like five minutes."

I stop painting my toes and look up. "That's it!"

Darcy pauses in her makeup application. "What?"

"That's my Story of the Year. It's perfect."

Chloe grabs a bottle of hairspray and squirts some on her bangs. "Rob's thought process is your story? Sounds like a short one."

"No, *guys*—how they think, what they really want, all the shit they do that makes no sense finally decoded and demystified. What girl wouldn't want to read that?" I'm getting so excited I knock the nail polish over and have to scramble to right it before it stains the tub. "It's socially relevant, right? Haven't women throughout the ages worried about this stuff?"

Darcy nods, thinking it over. "That is a good idea."

I scramble for my bag, grab a notebook and pen, and start scribbling. "We'll call it 'A Girl's Guide to Guys: Their Top Secrets Revealed.'"

"Ooh, I like it," Darcy says. "Very catchy! Except you should put in a number. You know how *Cosmo* always does that—'Top Ten Techniques for Better Orgasms,' that sort of thing?"

"Right! Good thinking. 'Their Top Seven Secrets Revealed.' How's that?"

"Not to be the voice of doom," Chloe says in a total voice-of-doom tone, "but what makes you think guys will just *volunteer* this information?"

"I'll do interviews—tonight! We can figure out what we most want to know, and I'll ask every guy at the party until I get some honest answers."

"Oh-kay"—Chloe draws the word out, all dubious and sarcastic—"but why would they tell you the truth?"

"Because I'm disarming." I smile my most disarming smile.

"You better hope nobody suspects you're Dr. Aphrodite, or they'll really clam up. Last I checked, most the guys at our school weren't terribly happy about that column."

"Yeah, but their major complaint is that I don't know how guys think, right?" I hold out my hands. "Here's their chance to explain. I'm all ears!"

Darcy rubs some gel into her pink hair and catches my eye in the mirror. "I think it's a great idea! I can't wait to hear what they say."

Chloe still looks unconvinced. "I've asked plenty of guys why they do what they do, and I've yet to get a straight answer."

"Yeah, but you can't be dating someone and expect him to be completely honest," I say. "There's too much at stake. Luckily, I'm not seeing anyone. None of these guys will care what I think."

"Except you'll go broadcasting the information to every girl on campus," Chloe says.

"It'll be *anonymous*. I'm a journalist—there's a strict code of ethics." I put the cap back on the nail polish even though I've only painted four of my toes. I'm too excited about this exposé to worry about grooming. I hold my pen over the paper, poised to strike. "Okay, so what do we most want to know?"

Darcy jumps right in. "When a guy says he's going to call and then just doesn't, what *is* that? If he's not going to call, why does he have to say he will? And what are we supposed to do about it? Pretend it doesn't bug us? Assume he'll call when he's ready? What?"

"Good!" I say, writing furiously. "Keep it coming."

"Ask about the every eight seconds thing," Chloe suggests.

I look at her blankly. "Every eight seconds?"

"Supposedly, guys think about sex every eight seconds. If that's true, how can they talk to their grandmothers? Gross!"

"Okay," I say, still writing, "I'll ask."

By eleven, Darcy's place is packed and the music is so loud you can feel it thrumming in every room. There's a keg out on the deck, a bunch of sophomore girls from the volleyball team are doing Jell-O shots in the kitchen, a gaggle of drama kids are playing beer pong in the basement, and the living room is just one huge dance floor. Darcy's a little buzzed and Chloe's working her way through her standard two drinks, sipped very slowly—more than that makes her feel out of control, which isn't something Chloe savors. I'm the only one among us who's stone-cold sober, though. I need to be clearheaded for my interviews.

I've read over the questions we came up with so many times, I've practically memorized them. I think they're pertinent. God knows I'd like them answered, not just for my article, but for my future relations with the opposite sex. That's assuming, of course, that I ever *have* relations; given the show of major male hostility on the message board today, my chances of finding a boyfriend in this town have dwindled from slim to miniscule.

1. When you say you're going to call and you don't, what happened?

2. Why are you so different when your friends are around? Which one is the real you?

3. What do you *really* look for in a girl?

4. Is it true that guys think about sex every eight seconds, or is that just a myth?

5. What's the surest way to tell the difference between a guy who's being sincere and one who's just looking to score?

6. What can make you lose interest in a girl overnight?

7. If you won't talk about your feelings, how are we supposed to know what they are?

I've been stalling, tell you the truth. The thought of actually approaching a guy and asking him these questions makes me feel a little queasy. Three hours ago, when I came up with the idea, it seemed so straightforward. I'd just go up to whoever and start firing away. What's so hard about conducting a few interviews? I'm not exactly shy. I mean, I've been doing theater forever. You can't get up onstage if you're self-conscious or inhibited, so this should be easy.

In the living room, I climb up onto an ottoman that's been shoved into a corner and look around. A huge mob of people are dancing, their shoes pounding on the hardwood floors as the bass beat throbs, rattling the framed prints on the walls. Darcy's dancing with Kevin Snodgrass, who's not exactly boyfriend material. He's what Chloe would call a POKSI (Physically Okay but Socially Inept). He's the sort of guy moms always want you to fall for, with his fastidious, perfectly parted blond hair, cherubic cheeks, and belted chinos. The Kevin Snodgrasses of the world are always nice, but hooking up with him would be like getting it on with your kid brother—too creepy. Hopefully, though, dancing with him is getting Darcy's mind off Rob, who had the nerve to show up with Michiko for fifteen minutes before Chloe and I made it clear they weren't welcome. What a jerk!

Okay, so who should be my first interviewee? Nathan Rease is over by the stereo, clutching a blue plastic cup, doing that little head bobbing thing guys do when they can't dance. He's in my math class; we studied for a test together one time. I could totally ask him. Of course, we'll have to find someplace quiet—maybe Darcy's room. But then he might think I'm coming on to him. When we studied together, there was this weird moment when we both reached for his calculator and our fingers touched and he stammered something about differential equations and I got the fleeting impression that he might have a tiny crush on me—just right then, never before or after—but still. It could be weird.

Right. Not Nathan, obviously.

Okay, how about Mick Matheson? He's never had a

crush on me, he's sweet, harmless and . . . time suckage personified. The boy could put a horde of rabid zombies to sleep with his monotone voice and bland, incredibly obvious observations. Yeah, that'll make for some scintillating reading. Not.

This is getting ridiculous! I'll never have my exposé by next Monday if I keep putting this off. Chas's and Rachel's smug faces pop into my mind. They think they're serious writers, real journalists with a future, whereas I'm just a chick churning out brain candy for the unsophisticated masses. How can I show them they're wrong unless I write something with real depth and insight? How can I even keep writing my column knowing how ignorant I am about the inner workings of guys? I've got to plow ahead and interview someone—anyone! Who cares who it is? I squeeze my eyes shut, wave my finger around, and point it randomly. When I open my eyes again, I'm staring right at Tony Brown.

And he's staring at me.

"What's up, Natalie?" Tony's a surfer with shaggy, unkempt hair and a boyish smile.

"Hey." Time to take the plunge. "Tony, can I ask you some questions?"

He leans closer. "Huh? Music's too loud."

"Yeah. Want to go outside?" I'm definitely not going into Darcy's bedroom with Tony Brown. Outside will have to do.

Tony waggles his eyebrows and follows me out the sliding glass doors to the deck. It's balmy out, the September heat lingering like it always does for the first few weeks of fall semester. I lead him to the corner farthest from the keg, where a couple deck chairs sit near the railing. I brush the leaves off one and sit. Tony yanks the other chair as close as he can to mine and drops into it, knees splayed, grinning.

"You look good tonight. That—what do you call it?" He gestures vaguely at my neckline.

"Um . . . halter top?"

"Halter top!" I can tell he's had a few beers. "Looks good on you."

"Oh, thanks." I'm glad it's dark enough out here to make my blush less obvious. "So, I'm working on this article? It's about, um, guys?" I can hear myself doing that annoying up-speak thing, turning statements into questions. I clear my throat.

"Yeah?" His smile looks forced now. "What about guys?"

"I'm trying to understand how they think and—you know—why they do what they do." I pull out my digital recorder. "Is it okay if I interview you?"

He shoots the recorder a suspicious glance. "I guess."

"Great!" I fish my notebook and pen from my purse, press RECORD, and smile at him with friendly interest. "Okay, first question: When you say you're going to call and you don't, what happened?"

He squints at me, confused. "I never told you I would call."

"No, not you and me—in general, say, if you were to tell a girl you'd call, and you didn't actually call her, what might be the reason for—"

"Did Jen put you up to this?"

Now it's my turn to look confused. "Jen?"

"I didn't promise I'd call her. Just because you ask for someone's number, it's not like you're engaged or anything." He takes a swig from his beer and scans the crowd around the keg.

"I'm not accusing you of anything! It's a hypothetical—"

"She's seeing Randy now anyway, so why should she care?"

I purse my lips, holding in my frustration. This isn't going well. He's obviously defensive. Maybe the questions are too accusatory? But I can't help it if the stuff we want to know is mostly about their maddening habits. I'll try a different angle; what's the least negative question? Something neutral.

"Forget that. It was stupid." I flash what I hope is an alluring smile and lean forward. "What do you *really* look for in a girl?"

His eyes dart toward my cleavage, which is pretty minimal, though the top I'm wearing makes the most of what I've got. "Uh, look for?"

"Yeah. Honestly. What do you find most attractive?"

The goofy, slightly buzzed grin he wore earlier returns. He looks at my hair. "I like brunettes. A lot. You've got great hair. It's so long and . . . shiny."

"Thanks. What else?"

He swallows. "I like a girl with long legs. Like yours. You ever think about modeling? You can make serious bank—"

"What about . . . you know . . . other qualities? Like personality-wise."

He frowns in concentration. "Well, I don't know you that well, but you seem really nice."

"Tony!" I cry in frustration. "This isn't about you and me or you and Jen, okay? It's research! Can't you just answer me honestly?"

He looks hurt for a second, then sudden understanding widens his eyes. "Ah, I see where you're going with this . . ."

"Yeah? So you'll be straight with me? No bullshit?"

"No bullshit."

I scan my list of questions and blurt out the first one that catches my eye. "Is it true that guys think about sex every eight seconds?"

He puts a hand on my knee. "Around you, more like every second."

"This isn't working," I say, pushing his hand off my leg.

"Natalie, you're cute. I like you. What more do we need? This whole interview thing is just getting in the way. Why

34

overthink it?" He leans forward, his lips moving in for the kill.

I jump to my feet. "Forget it!" I shove the recorder, notebook, and pen into my purse. "Forget I ever asked."

I push through the crowd around the keg and head to the bathroom. I don't really have to pee, but I need a moment to regroup after my disastrous first attempt at a serious interview. I close the door behind me and study my face in the mirror. Is there something about me that's sending the wrong signals? Maybe I shouldn't have worn this top.

I go to Darcy's room and find a light gray cardigan to put on over my halter top. Then I try on a pair of reading glasses she keeps by the bed. I check out the effect in the mirror. The glasses make me dizzy if I look through the lenses, but if I peer over the top of the frames I'm fine. A little less kegger bimbo, a little more serious reporter. Why not? My first technique bombed miserably, so this time I'm going to be all business.

As I'm making my way through the shadowy yard toward the house, I spot Kevin Snodgrass toting a bag of garbage outside. He tosses it in the big gray bin, then looks down at it regretfully.

"What's wrong?" My question makes him jump. "Sorry—didn't mean to startle you. What are you looking at?"

"Oh, nothing. I just know there's probably lots of recyclables in there. I should have sorted through it first."

I don't know whether to laugh or hug the poor guy; he's so earnest and sincere. Is that why he's also so unsexy, or is it the belted chinos? Maybe I should interview Kevin. Okay, so he's not exactly on Mountain View High's Most Desired list, but if anyone's going to cut the games and give it to me straight, it's him. I can start with pure-hearted, unsophisticated Kevin and work my way up to the sexier players once I've got my reporting chops down, right?

"Kevin, do you mind if I ask you a few questions?"

He pushes his glasses up onto the bridge of his nose and blinks at me owlishly. "About what?"

"Well, I'm working on an article about the way guys think. Would you help me out with an interview?" I concentrate on keeping my tone completely straightforward—no flirtation, no nothing, just what-you-see-is-what-you-get.

"Is it for a class?"

"Journalism. You know, for the school paper."

He shakes his head. "I'm sorry, Natalie, I'd like to help you out, but I don't think I can."

"Why not?"

"If you quote me as an expert or something, Brent and those guys might hassle me even more than they do now."

"Brent and those guys" translates as jocks. The kind of guys who are forever compelled to deposit the Kevin Snodgrasses of the world into garbage cans.

"It would be anonymous," I assure him. "I totally respect your need for privacy."

"Still, they might find out." He's already backing away from me. "Sorry."

"Wait, can't you just—?" But it's too late. He's already ducked inside.

Gawwwwd! What am I supposed to do? My potential sources either fear me or feel me up. All those guys who posted complaints about my cluelessness should witness this! Here I am, busting my butt to get a few measly insights, and you'd think I'm after classified information or something. I mean really, what the hell? Is being a guy so fascinating and controversial that they have to protect their trade secrets at any cost?

I hear the doorknob rattle on the back door before it flies open with extreme force. Chuck Hughes stumbles out, burping with such force it sounds painful. He zigzags unsteadily across the grass, obviously wasted. Chuck Hughes is always the super-trashed-puking-guy at every party. Ever since junior high, he's ended up in someone's bushes by midnight. Nobody ever invites him, but he's got bionic party-sensing powers; he can sniff out a keg from a hundred miles away.

Okay, I *really* don't feel like talking to Chuck Hughes, especially because of the potential puke factor, but watching him weave his way across the yard does give me an idea.

Tony wouldn't be straight with me because he had sex on the brain, and Kevin wouldn't talk because he didn't want to snitch. Maybe my best chance at honest dishing is with someone too inebriated to make a play or to fear the consequences. *In vino veritas,* right? So maybe in Budweiser there's a little truth too.

"Hey, Chuck," I call. "Come over here a second, will you?"

He stops his loopy waltz across the lawn and looks around, confused. "Huh?"

I walk up to him, eager to get this over with. If I wait for his damaged brain cells to locate me and command his legs to carry him in my direction, it could take hours.

"What's up?" I'm going for home-girl casual this time.

"Natalie," he says, stumbling over the syllables. "How you?"

"Not bad. Listen, I want to ask you something, okay?"

He makes a gun with his fingers. "Shoot."

"What's the surest way to tell the difference between a guy who's being sincere and one who's just looking to score?"

He sways unsteadily for a long moment, blank-faced.

I wait as long as I can stand to wait. "Chuck? Did you hear me?"

"Sorry, whaz the question?"

I repeat myself, enunciating so clearly I feel like an ESL teacher. Again, he just stands there, looking like a stunned bear in the moonlight. Finally he rubs his face. "Yeah. Okay. We'll pretend this never happened."

"Wait, what? It's a question. Can't you just answer it?" My tone has gone from home-girl to strained patient to totally irritated.

He points an accusing finger in my direction and bellows, "You trying to take advantage of me! Just because I'm wasted doesn't mean I'm stupid!"

I throw my hands up. "Whatever!"

I storm back into the house, searching through one crowded room after another for Darcy or Chloe. I need a reality check here. What the hell am I doing wrong? What are these guys so scared of revealing? That's when I feel a cool hand on my arm.

"Natalie! It is you. Didn't recognize you at first in those glasses."

I turn to see Summer Sheers and hastily take off the borrowed specs. She's wearing a pink tube top, a short skirt, and her signature shoes: high-heeled pale brown Dolce & Gabbana boots. Her mounds of glossy blond hair are meant to look windblown and tousled but have obviously been meticulously arranged over her tan, luminous shoulders. Her lips are so coated in lip gloss it looks like she just polished off a whole tub of fried chicken.

"Hey, Summer."

She smiles an innocent, sympathetic smile. "I didn't

know you had vision problems. That must be a drag."

I shrug. "I was just trying them out. How's the play going?"

Summer's in *The Importance of Being Earnest* at the boys' prep school just outside of town, Underwood Academy. Tons of girls from our school auditioned for only three roles; Darcy, Chloe, and Summer got cast. It's a pretty rare opportunity to meet guys from Underwood, who are rumored to be cuter, smarter, and way more chivalrous than the losers at our school. I didn't even try out. We did the same play last year at our high school, and I got stuck as Summer's understudy. Despite learning every single line and fervently praying she'd get a bad case of dysentery, I never even got to perform. That's when I decided to stop focusing on theater and start pouring more energy into my writing.

"Oh, it's great!" she gushes. "I'm learning so much. It's amazing how much more in depth you can go when you play the same role a second time. Plus the guys at Underwood are so hot! Why didn't you audition? You already know all the lines."

My stomach churns. "I knew you'd get it."

She slaps my shoulder playfully. "Nuh-uh!"

"Obviously. You're great in that role."

I despise the rituals of fake friendship Summer and I enact whenever we meet. I wish we could just claw each other's eyes out and call it a day; instead we put on huge, radiant smiles and spout compliments until my teeth hurt from the saccharine sweetness of it all.

"Oh, I think you'd do it beautifully," she says. "We've got to get you back on the stage. I heard we're doing *A Midsummer Night's Dream* in the spring. Won't that be fun? You would be an amazing Titania."

Translation: *You don't stand a chance.*

"We'll see . . ." I hope my enigmatic grin masks my murderous impulses. "Oh, you better get in line for that keg. Looks like it's running out."

She swivels toward the keg crowd and I make my escape.

This party is turning out to be the turd-encrusted cherry on the top of my shit-shake of a day.

●●●●●●●●●●●●●●●●●●

Chapter Four

●●●●●●●●●●●●●●●●●●

"*C*ome on!" Darcy spoons batter onto the waffle iron and laughs. "It couldn't have been that bad."

"Oh, it was worse!" I've just finished recapping my disastrous foray into investigative reporting. "The whole night was a total bust. Either they told me what they thought I wanted to hear, or they were suspicious and clammed up. Nobody said anything worth writing down."

It's almost two in the afternoon on Saturday, and we've finally finished cleaning Darcy's house, erasing all signs of the party so her parents won't freak when they come home Sunday night. Now we're finally getting around to breakfast. I'm washing and slicing the strawberries while Darcy makes waffles and Chloe brews another pot of French press Sumatra.

"Call me crazy," Chloe says, "but maybe a kegger isn't the most scientific environment for research."

I wave this concern away. "If they're not comfortable telling me the truth after a couple beers, they sure as hell won't open up anywhere else. No, I don't think the environment was the problem."

"So maybe it's your technique." Chloe's always eager to offer a little brutal honesty.

"Maybe, but I doubt it. I tried all kinds of approaches: sexy, friendly, intimidating—nothing worked. I'm starting to think there's an invisible force field that prevents honest communication between X and Y chromosomes."

The waffle iron beeps and Darcy opens it, impales the waffle, deposits it on a plate. "Chloe, you take this one. If you get too hungry you'll be bitchy."

"Don't you mean bitchier?" I correct.

Chloe shoots me an evil look and takes the plate from Darcy. She smothers it in strawberries and syrup, pours herself more coffee, jumps up on the counter beside me, and digs in. I watch, envious, breathing in the sublime smell.

"Oh, and to make things worse, I had a delightful conversation with Summer." I make my voice all fluttery like hers. "'It's so *amazing* playing Cecily again! It's just *amazing* what you can learn when you do the same role twice.' I was like *excuse me, I just puked inside my mouth.*"

Chloe swallows hard and glowers at me. "Hello! Some of us are eating."

"I wish you were in the show with us instead of her," Darcy says. "You should have auditioned! You totally would have gotten it."

"She didn't last time," Chloe says.

"Thanks!" I bump her with my shoulder.

Chloe holds up a hand. "You didn't let me finish! I was going to say you didn't get it last time *because* you let Malibu Barbie psyche you out. She's not half the actress you are and you know it."

"Being in a show at Underwood is so fun, Natalie." Darcy's tone is sincere—she's not rubbing it in, just telling it straight. "The campus is gorgeous and their theater's so big. Their guys are better actors too."

"It's true. Plus they're much more hygienic." Chloe licks the syrup from her lips. "I challenge you to find anyone half as perfect for me as Josh. He's so polished."

"And clean," I remind her.

Darcy giggles. "He's almost as anal as her."

"What is it with you people?" she scolds. "First 'puke,' now 'anal.' You know how sensitive my gag reflex is."

Chloe has an incredibly weak stomach. In the sixth grade, when we got a perfunctory lecture on menstruation from Mrs. O'Malley, Chloe threw up. There have been countless other incidents over the years. Just about any mention of bodily fluids or the digestive process sets her off.

"Maybe you could go to rehearsal with us sometime at

least," Darcy suggests. "I know you'd love the campus. And the guys. You ready for your waffle?"

I just sit there, blinking at her. I'm getting an idea. A wonderful, awful idea.

"Natalie?" Darcy asks. "You okay?"

"Why didn't I think of this before?" I spring off the counter and do an impromptu Snoopy dance. "Oh, God, it's brilliant! It's so perfect!"

"What?" they ask in unison.

"Underwood! I'll get my story at Underwood!"

Darcy tilts her head sideways. "You'll interview guys there?"

"Why would they tell you any more than the ones you talked to last night?" Chloe asks.

"Because I won't interview them as a girl." I lower my voice to a dramatic whisper and lean toward them. "I'll go undercover . . . as a guy!"

I wait for this to sink in. As it does, their eyes light up and all three of us start cackling madly like the witches from *Macbeth*, the second carafe of Sumatra and my brilliant idea hitting our systems simultaneously.

"It's so Shakespeare!" Darcy cries, clapping her hands. "Like when you played Portia in *The Merchant of Venice*, remember?"

"Wait, you're not seriously considering . . . ?" Chloe trails off.

"I can pull it off, right?" I glance down at my chest. I'm wearing a T-shirt, no bra, and there's very little there to write home about. "It's not like my ample breasts will get in the way."

"It's so James Bond!" Darcy twirls around like a little girl. "Undercover! Secret agents! We can have code names and communicate via walkie-talkie."

"Cell phones might be less conspicuous, 007." Chloe rolls her eyes, already recovering from her brief brush with enthusiasm and returning to her natural state of bitchy skepticism. "Hold on, though. How are you going to get in? Even if they believe you're a guy, it's not like you can just enroll. You've got to apply and stuff, don't you?"

That stops us all for a moment.

"I have an idea," Darcy says. "This is probably unethical, but my cousin Granger is a seriously accomplished hacker. I bet he could get into their system."

"Would we have to pay him?" I ask.

She scoffs. "It's all he does. He lives for it. He's twelve and he has access to FBI files! I'll see if he can fix it so they'll think you're a new student."

"We'd have to move on it fast," I say. "The deadline's coming up."

She pulls her cell from her pocket. "I'm on it."

"So we're really doing this?" My voice edges up in excitement.

"Hold on, hold on." Chloe puts a hand up. "How are you going to miss school without anyone noticing?"

"I don't have to be gone long. A week, tops."

"What about your mom? Everyone at Underwood lives there, you know. You can't just go home at night. Won't your mom get worried if you're missing for days on end?"

"She can say she's staying with me," Darcy puts in. "I'll cover for her."

"And homework?" Chloe demands.

"You guys can get me my assignments and I'll make it up later."

Chloe purses her lips, considering. I bump my hip against hers playfully.

"Come on! You know you love it. If I pull this off we'll be legendary."

"Hmm . . . I don't know."

"Where's your spirit of adventure?" I ask. "It's a madcap scheme full of intrigue and danger! What's not to love?"

"Umm . . . the fact that it's completely misguided and insane?"

"Exactly! That's what's so great about it. So are we doing this, or what?"

"I'm in," Darcy says without hesitation.

Chloe's lips curve into a reluctant grin. "It's twisted and

probably doomed to failure, but if you're determined, I guess I have no choice."

I squeal and jump around while Darcy calls her cousin.

If we really want to pull this off we'll have to haul ass. Story of the Year entries are due at five o'clock a week from Monday. That means I have to get in, get out, and get the thing written in eight days. Even though my rehearsal time is tighter than usual, especially for such a demanding role, I'm kind of glad. This has to do with what I call the eating-insects-on-a-dare principle. The crazier the idea, the less time you can afford to spend thinking about it. If I hesitate to consider all the possible ways this stunt can go horribly askew, I'll never have the nerve to show up at Underwood Monday morning. It's now or never.

Saturday night Darcy, Chloe, and I talk strategy over Chinese takeout and Diet Coke. Darcy's cousin Granger is all over the hacking challenge. He's promised to call as soon as he's made headway. In the meantime, we've got our work cut out for us. I make a quick to-do list in my notebook:

1. Extreme makeover: haircut, etc.
2. Vocal training: lowered voice,
typical male speech patterns

3. Costume: assemble suitable boy
clothes until uniform can be obtained
4. Body language: walk, gestures,
handshakes, spitting
5. Plan for absence: Decide how to
keep normal life at bay for one week

"At last," Darcy says when she sees number one on my list. "I've been dying to cut your hair for ages!"

Oh, God. I feel a little sick to my stomach as she pulls me toward her room. Chloe trails after us with a stack of *Vogue*s. Darcy produces her gleaming silver scissors, holds them close to her face, and slices the air a couple of times dramatically like a serial killer testing her weapon of choice.

"You can't escape, my pretty," Chloe cries in her Wicked Witch voice.

Darcy creeps toward me, scissors outstretched.

I back away. "Lots of guys have long hair, right?"

"Not the boys at Underwood," Darcy says.

"Couldn't I just . . . wear a hat?"

She stops stalking me abruptly and lowers her chin to give me a look. "Are you committed to this role?"

"I'm committed! I am." I swallow my instincts and scramble over to the little cushioned stool before Darcy's dressing table.

Darcy puts on her black hairdresser's PVC apron. (I'm serious—she's way into this stuff. If she doesn't make it as a famous character actress, she will definitely be hair-dresser to the stars.) She tucks her scissors into the pocket and stands behind me. Running her fingers through my hair in a professional manner she studies my reflection in the mirror.

"Hmm," she says, cocking her head this way and that.

Chloe holds up a picture from *Vogue* of a runway model with a shaved head. "I think we should go all the way."

I cringe. I'm not obsessed with my looks or anything, but I do have certain strengths in the beauty department. I've got great legs, big hazel eyes, a full mouth, and long, shiny hair. Of those four assets, I have to say it's my hair I'm most attached to. I guess that's because my body is already so boyish, what with the total lack of hips and barely there boobs, that my hair is hands down the most feminine thing about me. Without it, I really will look like a boy.

Of course, that's the whole point. Still, I can't help but feel like we're about to amputate the girl right out of me.

"Don't worry," Darcy chuckles. "This is going to look awesome."

"We're not shaving it, right?"

Chloe holds up another picture, one of a male model with slightly choppy short hair. "More like this, maybe?"

Darcy turns and studies the photo. "Uh-huh. That's

good. Really short in the back and sides, with a little more fullness through the top. We could throw some highlights through the front—"

"No highlights," I say. "Just the cut."

Darcy shrugs. "You're the boss."

She grabs a spray bottle and wets my hair with one hand, combing it carefully with the other, all the while studying me from various angles with a look of intense concentration.

I close my eyes. "God, just do it."

"Relax. It grows back."

"I know, I know. It's just—"

A snipping sound stops me mid-sentence. My eyes fly open. A huge shank of hair is missing from the right side of my head. I squeeze my eyes shut again. "Oh, God."

Chloe says in the Moviefone voice, *"She was a woman, struggling to know the hearts of men . . ."*

Darcy swivels the stool around so I can't see myself in the mirror. "It'll be easier this way. Trust me."

None of us say anything for a little while, and the only sound in the room is the rhythmic snip-snip-snip of the scissors mixed with the light flick of paper as Chloe flips through *Vogue*. I gaze into the soulful, tortured eyes of Jim Morrison as his various incarnations assess me from the ceiling and walls. He offers no comment.

"It'll be liberating, right?" I say to no one in particular.

"Guys have it so easy. They don't really worry about how they look. They just spray on a little Axe and go."

Chloe snorts. "Not all of them. I've dated guys who spend more time on their hair than I do."

I press on, undeterred, trying to convince myself as my shiny hair piles up on the floor. "In general, though, they're less neurotic than we are, don't you think? They worry less. Short hair will be my first step toward experiencing male power and freedom."

"Yeah," Darcy says. "You'll get to know what it's like to live hairspray-free."

"Just don't become a gel addict," Chloe warns. "That's not a good look."

After an interminable wait, Darcy says, "You ready for this? Step one in male-ification: makeover magic." She spins me around on the swivel stool so I'm facing the mirror again. "Ta-dah!"

The girl in the mirror instantly freaks me out. It's me, but it's not me. The glossy waves around my face are now gone. What's left stands up from my scalp in boyish disarray. I stare, unable to speak.

"Say something," Darcy urges me. "Do you love it? I love it."

Chloe appears beside her in the mirror, her smile huge. "Nice work, Paul Mitchell! Gorgeous."

"I—wow—it's really . . . short," I finally manage.

Chloe says, "Jeez, Nat. Don't take this the wrong way, but I think I'm kind of attracted to you."

Darcy tousles my damp hair playfully. "God, it's so flattering! Your eyes look enormous."

It's true. With all that hair gone, there's nothing to hide behind. My cheekbones are more pronounced, my eyes wider, my lips fuller and pinker. I'm all . . . face.

"I'm such a genius," Darcy muses happily. "Now if only I could get you to pierce your nose . . ."

Darcy's cell chirps and she reaches under her apron to fish it from the pocket of her jeans. She glances at the display before answering. "Granger? What do you got?"

Chloe and I lock eyes in the mirror while Darcy paces around with the phone, going "uh-huh" and "right" and "okay." It reminds me of waiting for a cast list to be posted, fidgeting helplessly as the thing I've been obsessing over is about to be unveiled.

Darcy finally presses a button and puts her phone back in her pocket. I swivel around to face her; Chloe and I both stare at her expectantly. For a terrifying moment her expression is so serious I know it didn't work and we've just mutilated my hair for no reason.

Then she breaks into a glorious smile. "He did it! You're in."

Chloe squeals.

"Really?" My heart's racing. "How? What did he do?"

She holds up her hands. "The kid's a little Einstein, man. I don't ask for details. All I know is your name's Nat Rodgers and they should be expecting you in the Admissions office Monday morning."

It's really happening. We're actually doing this. I feel sick and amazed and thrilled all at once. Operation Babe in Boyland is officially launched.

●●●●●●●●●●●●●●●●●
Chapter Five
●●●●●●●●●●●●●●●●●

$\mathscr{S}$unday morning we drive to Corte Madera to shop for my disguise. Luckily, Underwood has a uniform, so I just need one basic guy outfit to get me through the door. I've been practicing speaking in a low, manly voice, using my breath the way our drama teacher taught me back when I played Portia's cross-dressing scene. In the car on the way to the mall Chloe and Darcy agree it's a passably convincing register for Nat.

"No matter what, though, you can't slip into your normal girl voice," Darcy warns. "You've got to keep it guy-like all the time."

Chloe puts on her blinker and steers her Honda toward the mall. "Maybe Nat should be shy. If you don't say much, you're less likely to get caught."

"Yeah, but then will I really get answers?" I ask. "You think just being there, I'll magically understand all there is to know about them? Won't I have to get, you know, chummy?"

"Ooh!" Chloe says, parking her car in a shady spot. "You've got to find out if Josh likes me! He's so yum!"

"I'm not doing this so I can fix you up with Mr. Clean," I grumble.

"Why are you doing it, then?" She yanks her keys from the ignition and touches up her lipstick in the rearview mirror.

"To create a deeper understanding between the sexes," I say. "To answer the questions girls have asked about guys since time began."

She twists around to look at me in the backseat. "Well, I'm a girl, and I have a question: Does Josh like me?"

"Fine," I say, opening the car door. "I'll see what I can find out."

In Macy's, Chloe gets distracted by the shoe department, but we remind her sternly we don't have time for cute fall boots. We make our way to men's clothing. Aside from passing through en route to the bathroom, I've never even visited this department; it's totally foreign. As we're looking at button-down shirts a paunchy, middle-aged man with thinning hair approaches and asks if he can help us find anything.

"We're shopping for her twin brother," Darcy says, pointing at me. "She's going to try some stuff on, just to make sure it all fits. Him, I mean. Fits him. Nat. Her brother."

"All right, excellent," the man says. "Let me know if I can be of help." His face clearly says, *Damn kids.*

In the dressing room, we get the giggles at the way the jeans hang below my butt crack. When I find some that are baggy enough to be guy-like but not so loose that they'll end up around my ankles, we pair them with a plain white button-down shirt. At their insistence, I walk up and down the hall outside the dressing room a couple times while they coach me on how to move.

"You've got to slouch more," Darcy says. "Your posture's too femmie."

Chloe nods. "Think gangsta, you know? Lean down into it."

I try, but they're still not satisfied. An old guy comes out of a dressing room carrying a bunch of sweaters and scowling at us, which sets us off giggling again. When we recover I resume my practice walk, but even I can see in the mirror that it's not convincing. Something's off, but I can't put a finger on it. Chloe studies me, shaking her head, then suddenly her face lights up with inspiration.

"I know what you need!"

"What?" I recognize that gleam in her eye, so I'm instantly suspicious.

"It's all a matter of props. Darcy, go get us a pair of socks."

"Socks?" Her forehead scrunches up in confusion.

"Hurry!"

Darcy runs out and in a few minutes she comes back with a pair of black cotton socks. "Does it matter what size they are?"

Chloe just laughs at that and hands the socks to me. "Here you go. Instant junk."

I raise an eyebrow. "You want me to stuff it down my pants?"

"Yeah! Remember, you've got a package down there now."

I glance around quickly to make sure nobody's around, then stuff the pair of socks into the appropriate spot— more or less, anyway. It occurs to me that I'm not completely confident about placement. I mean, obviously I'm familiar enough with male anatomy to know the basics, but I never really thought about how they arrange it under clothing—how it hangs, so to speak. Once more I check to make sure nobody's come into the dressing room, then I adjust the socks, examining their barely visible outline in the mirror.

"You can hardly see it," I say. "You really think it's necessary?"

Chloe breathes out the long-suffering sigh of someone forced to interact with people of vastly inferior intelligence. "It's not about the bulge; it's about the way it *feels*. Go ahead, try the walk again."

I do, and before I've even taken three steps Darcy gasps. "God! That's it! Chloe, you're a genius."

She's right. I can feel the difference, see it in the mirror. There's just something about having that bulge between my legs that makes me move more convincingly. I might not have the manliest strut on the planet, but it will definitely pass.

Chloe nods. "By George, I think you've got it."

I laugh and walk around some more, enjoying my new macho competence. "I always wondered what that expression meant."

They both look at me, puzzled. "What expression?" Darcy asks.

"Cock of the walk."

They groan in unison at my bad joke.

As they hang up clothes and debate which ones I should get, I turn back to my reflection for one last look. It's so weird how the person staring back at me is familiar and yet isn't Natalie, almost like I really am looking at my long-lost twin. For the first time since we decided to attempt this crazy stunt, Nat Rodgers seems real to me. He seems like a person I can try to become.

We stroll through the outdoor mall sipping iced coffee drinks. Mine is a caramel-soy latte, Darcy's got a java chip Frappuccino, and Chloe takes hers black. The sunshine is warm on my head and face. I decide I really like my new short hair—it's lighter, cooler, easier. It looks good too; even in my ratty T-shirt and jeans I catch two or three guys checking me out, which is nice. Their glances, along with the gorgeous blue sky, my loyal girls, and the caffeine rush, boost my overall confidence in the rightness of the world.

"So you're going to tell your mom you're at my house, right?" Darcy asks.

I nod. "Seems like the best plan."

"Doing what, though?" Darcy's muses, twisting her straw in circles.

I take another sip of latte and consider. "Maybe we could say we have a huge project due at school and it'll require super-long hours. I'll say we procrastinated or something."

"The old 'homework' excuse, huh?" Chloe says. "You think she'll buy it?"

"Maybe, maybe not. I can't think of anything else, though. If she calls, of course, Darcy will have to cover." I turn to Darcy. "And keep her from talking to your parents. That might be tricky."

Darcy nods. "It's not perfect, but I guess it'll have to do. Luckily, your mom's not as control freaky as most."

"Yeah," I say, "and she's actually really busy at work right now, so she might be distracted enough not to get suspicious. I'll tell her after, I guess—I mean when I write the article. Maybe I'll wait to see if it wins, though. If it doesn't, she might never have to know."

"What about the school?" Chloe brushes a strand of hair from her eyes. "Don't they send out e-mails now to parents if you miss classes?"

I nod. "Yeah, but the account they have on file is an old one she never checks, so that's okay. Plus I know her username and password, so I could get in there and delete it just to be safe."

I know this makes me sound really devious, but I try to convince myself deception and scheming are excusable this one time. I'm doing it for girls everywhere, not just for me. Mom's a lawyer, a total powerhouse career woman who takes women's rights very seriously. I think she'd be proud of my pioneering spirit, but if I reveal what I have planned she'll feel obligated as a parent to stop me. I mean, it's one thing to support gender-bending experiments in theory, but quite another to tell your only daughter she can skip school for a week and live amongst hundreds of hormone-crazed males disguised as one of them. She'd support it philosophically, but I can't risk telling her since I'm pretty sure she'd forbid it. I'm keeping her in the dark for her own good, since even if she did let me go, she'd proceed to worry herself sick all week.

Chloe stops walking and nearly chokes on her coffee.

I pat her back. "You okay?"

"Don't look now, but I just saw Josh Mayer coming out of Abercrombie and Fitch."

Darcy's head swings around. "Where?"

"I said don't look!" Chloe hisses.

"Who?" I ask, confused.

"Josh Mayer!" Darcy says too loudly.

Chloe clamps a hand over Darcy's mouth and says to me, "The hottie from Underwood I told you about?"

"Oh, *scheisse*!" Instinctively I duck. "He can't see me or we're screwed."

Chloe's eyes widen. "You're right! Hide in a store. We'll text you when the coast is clear. Darcy, come with me."

Darcy looks over her shoulder again. "Where?"

"To go flirt with him, of course!" Chloe arranges her bangs and applies fresh lip gloss. "Hurry, Natalie! He's headed our way."

I keep my head low and dart into the nearest store, an upscale kids' clothing boutique. The lady behind the counter is talking to an extremely pregnant woman. As I burst in, casting furtive glances over my shoulder, they offer raised eyebrows followed by wooden, strained smiles.

"Can I help you?" the saleslady asks.

"No, um, just looking!"

After an awkward silence, I edge my way over to the floor-to-ceiling windows and peek around a rocking horse. There's Chloe, tossing her hair, laughing. She's talking to the guy who must be Josh. I can only see him in profile, but I have to admit he does look pretty damn beautiful. He has flawless skin, bright blue eyes, and long, ropey muscles that bulge under his thin yellow T-shirt. His dark blond hair is meticulously arranged to look ever so slightly boy-band messy.

Darcy stands nearby, outside their orbit, studying her Frappuccino with intense concentration. I feel kind of bad for her. I know what it's like to be Chloe's wingman when she's working it—how abruptly you can feel invisible. I don't blame Chloe for turning her full attention on this Josh character, though. Wow. He's one of the prettiest guys I've ever seen in real life. If all the guys at Underwood look like that, I'll need a bib to catch my drool.

"Natalie! What a surprise."

I turn to see Summer Sheers watching me with a bemused expression. She's wearing an olive green dress with her D&G boots, looking fresh and radiant as ever. Beside her is a slightly older version of herself—equally blond, equally skinny, equally dewy and ethereal, but twenty-something instead of sixteen.

"Summer!" I squeak. "Hey."

Summer gestures at the girl beside her. "This is my sister, Autumn."

"Nice to meet you." I shake her hand.

"Same here." Autumn smiles politely before drifting over to the infant clothes.

"We're shopping for a baby shower. What are *you* doing here?" Summer tries to see past me to the scene outside.

I block her view. "Nothing."

"Nothing, huh?" She doesn't look even remotely convinced.

"I just really love baby clothes." I grab the nearest item—a god-awful little dress in garish lime green chiffon, and jerk it around like a headless puppet. "So cute!"

"Mm," she says doubtfully. "Wow, your hair is . . . short."

My hand shoots up to yank on my bangs. "Yep."

"What inspired that?"

Scheisse! Summer's the last person I need suspecting anything. Not only is she my total nemesis, she's also in the play at Underwood. She could screw everything up, and would no doubt love every second of it. "Just wanted a change."

Outside, Chloe explodes in laughter, and Summer's eyes drift again to the window. "Oh my God, Josh Mayer's out there!"

I throw a quick look over my shoulder. "Oh. Yeah."

"Do you know Josh? No, I guess you probably don't. Come outside with me and I'll introduce you. He's so nice. All the guys at Underwood are *amazing*."

"No thanks," I say too quickly.

Her eyes narrow. "Didn't you come here with Chloe and Darcy?"

Scheisse, scheisse, scheisse! "Yeah . . ."

"But you're in here"—she looks around—"and they're out there?"

A high-pitched trumpet of laughter escapes my pursed lips. "We're not attached at the hip! Like I said, I just *love* baby clothes. Plus I saw something in the window that would be so perfect for my nephew."

"Oh yeah?" She tries to make it sound like friendly interest, but I can see the wheels turning in her head. "What?"

I look around and seize on the closest item without frills. "This! Isn't it great?" My hand lands on the butt of the rocking horse in the window. The horse rolls forward, bumping its nose on the window noisily, making the plate glass rattle. The women at the counter shoot me alarmed glances.

"Something I can show you?" calls the one at the register.

"Not just yet." I waggle my fingers in apology. "Still deciding."

"For your nephew, huh?" Summer says, eyebrows arched. "I thought you were an only child."

"I call him my nephew. Because we're so close. Really he's my third cousin once removed. Something like that."

Summer looks out the window again. "Oh! Josh is leaving. Maybe I'll run out and say hi. Sure you don't want to—?"

"No, go on! Really."

She shoots me one last calculating look, obviously trying to figure out what's up, but the lure of Hot Josh proves stronger than her curiosity. I crouch behind the rocking horse again and peek over its butt to watch. She floats over to them, blond hair bouncing. Josh has already started toward the parking lot. Summer calls out a greeting and Josh turns, waves, makes a gesture of apology, then keeps going.

Finally! I breathe a sigh of relief but wait until he's turned the corner before I venture out.

As I approach, Summer's saying, "You two ready for tech week? It's going to be grueling. Late rehearsals every night. I can't believe we open Friday."

Chloe looks bored. "I'm sure we'll manage."

"It'll be fun," she trills. "Well, I better get back to Autumn before she gets mad."

"Autumn?" Darcy asks, looking around.

"My sister. See you tomorrow!"

As she flounces back into the boutique Chloe mumbles, "Who the hell names their kids Summer and Autumn?"

"People whose offspring have agents before they're potty trained," Darcy replies.

"I know, right?" Chloe shakes her head. "Did you hear her talking about this big audition she has coming up? Some big movie? Like she's even that good! Her dad's just well connected."

"I don't like that she saw me," I say, keeping my voice low. "I don't like it at all."

Darcy says, "Why shouldn't she?"

I tug at my hair. "She was already suspicious. She'll be at Underwood every night this week. If she catches me there the whole plan is dead in the water."

Chloe winces. "I didn't think of that."

"We'll have to keep her away from you." Darcy pats my arm. "Don't worry. How could she possibly guess what we're up to?"

"She has ESB," I say.

Chloe rolls her eyes. "ESP you mean?"

"No, ESB. Extrasensory Bitchyness."

They both laugh. We slurp the last of our coffee and toss the plastic cups. As we make our way back to Chloe's car I tell myself it's all going to be fine: I'm going to perfect my disguise, write a fabulous article, learn all about the inner workings of boys, and prove myself as a serious journalist. Nobody's going to get in my way, certainly not Summer Sheers. It's all going to work out just great.

Really.

Chapter Six

*A*s I drive my Buick to Underwood Monday morning I feel seriously nauseous. I can't stop chanting *What am I doing? What am I doing?* over and over as I maneuver through the familiar streets. Our plan seems deeply delusional in the brilliant morning sunlight.

At least my mom seemed to buy the school project story when I sprang it on her last night. She's so busy right now with a huge civil rights case, I suspect the idea of not having to worry about dinners for a whole week made her eager to believe. She's not a bad mom, just super into her career. Dad hasn't been on the scene since I was a baby, so she's had to keep us afloat, which couldn't have been easy.

Actually, having no dad is part of what makes me extra-nervous about infiltrating Underwood. If I'd grown up with a father or at least brothers in my life I'd know *something* about living with guys. As it is, I'm like Dorothy walking right into the Emerald City—absolutely clueless.

I reach down and adjust my sock nervously. It's stuffed into my new BVDs, and in some weird way touching it is reassuring. Like a talisman or something. Okay, that's just weird.

"Hello," I say in my deepest voice, "I'm Nat Rodgers."

It sounds okay. The double layer of sports bras strapping down my boobs feels so tight, though, like they're cutting off my circulation. I'm wearing a blazer over my button-down shirt, and the autumn heat is getting to me. I pause at a red light and roll down the window, yanking at my collar.

I study myself in the rearview mirror. It's so weird, going out in public with absolutely no makeup. I'm not one of those girls who slathers on an inch of foundation every day, but I usually wear mascara and lip gloss, at least. I feel kind of exposed, going without, but obviously I don't want anything calling attention to my big eyes and full lips, which are already girly enough to arouse suspicion, I'm afraid.

I try out my Nat voice again. "Hey! What's up? I'm Nat. How's it hanging? Oh yeah? She's cute. I'd do that in a heartbeat."

A horn blares at me, followed by another, and I jump. Apparently the light turned green while I was shooting the shit with my mirror.

"Jeez, calm down!" I put the Buick in gear and cruise west, my face burning with embarrassment.

I've never been to Underwood before, even though it's only about ten minutes from town. I follow the signs, which lead me higher and higher on a twisty, tree-lined road.

Suddenly the road levels out and the tangle of disorderly forest gives way to a long paved driveway. It seems to go on and on. Birch trees line up like sentries on either side of the dark ribbon of road, their pale branches and silvery leaves casting dappled shadows on my dirty windshield. Beyond them stretches an impeccably manicured lawn.

I pass a large brass sign that says UNDERWOOD ACADEMY and my heart starts pounding so hard I can feel it in my throat. I turn another corner and the main building looms large before me, drawing from me a small, involuntary gasp. It's like nothing I've ever seen outside of the movies. The stone walls reach up and up, half obscured by tangled ivy. The windows are tall as a grown man and elegantly arched. Gothic spires point straight up at the clouds like proud, accusing fingers. It couldn't be more intimidating.

I pull into a parking lot right behind the main building. The trappings of big money are hard to miss: I spot a Jag, a convertible Mercedes, a black BMW, a brand-new canary yellow Ferrari. The cars gleam in the morning sun, their paint jobs still so bright and new they hurt my eyes. You'll find some sweet cars in the parking lot of Mountain View

70

High, sure, but here nearly every vehicle looks crazy posh and fresh off the showroom floor. My 1960 Buick LeSabre, a kitschy old relic I inherited from my mom, sticks out even worse than usual here.

I can hear the crunch of gravel on tires as more cars drive up, doors slam, male voices call out greetings. All the students at Underwood live here, but some of them go home on weekends. Everyone's wearing uniforms: navy blue blazers and pants, crisp white shirts, red ties.

"Oh my God," I whisper. "What am I doing?" My palms are slick and the blazer I'm wearing is stifling—I can feel big wet patches forming under my arms.

I remember all the times my adrenaline spiked as I stood in the wings, waiting to go onstage. I'd try to think of my first line, but my brain would be blank as a fresh sheet of paper. Then my cue would come and I'd force my legs to propel me into the hot glare of the stage lights. I'd hear my own voice saying my line and the sick churning storm inside my belly would go dead calm, smooth as glass. This is just like that, right? It's scary now, but as soon as I'm saying my lines I'll be fine.

A tap on my window makes me yelp. I whip around and see a guy about my age standing there in an Underwood uniform, studying me with interest. Oh, Jesus, that was not a manly sound that just escaped me. Did he hear? Cautiously, I roll down my window.

"Hi. Are you Nat Rodgers?"

"Yeah," I squeak, then lower my voice a couple octaves. "Who wants to know?"

He shoots me a curious look. "The headmaster told me I should keep an eye out for you. When I saw this car, I figured it might be you. You're new, right?"

"Yeah."

"Great! I'm supposed to show you around. I'm Tyler Woodrow." He reaches a hand through the window, which I shake awkwardly, hoping he doesn't notice my clammy palms. "Student body treasurer, MMORPG enthusiast. You a gamer?"

"Not really." I smile weakly and get out of the car. It's now officially impossible for me to turn around and pretend this whole plan never happened. I'm here now. It's definitely happening.

"Welcome to Underwood. I've been watching the parking lot, hoping I'd catch you. It's unusual to start this late, but don't worry, I can answer any questions you might have."

Chloe would definitely dub Tyler a POKSI. I know that's kind of mean, but my social radar tells me immediately the label fits. He reminds me of Kevin Snodgrass—he's got that earnest, cherubic quality that moms love but everyone else sees as decidedly uncool. He's got brown hair parted neatly and combed way too carefully. We're about the same height, probably the same age, but something about his eager, open expression and his clear gray eyes make him look way younger. I guess in junior high he missed the memo about developing a cynical distrust of the world in general, and he's never really caught up since.

I study his face for signs of *Oh my God you're a girl,* but can't find any. He just returns my gaze, placid and accepting. He peers into the backseat where I've put my stuff. Darcy lent me her plain black duffel bag; we decided my bright pink polka-dotted luggage might attract attention.

"You can leave your stuff here for now," he says. "We'll come back and get it before I take you to the dorms. Ready for our first stop? The headmaster wants to see you before class." He glances at his watch. "We'd better hurry."

The headmaster's office has polished wood floors, pale walls, and an art deco lamp suspended from the ceiling. A very thin woman with an enormous confection of hair sits behind an old-fashioned wooden desk, a computer angled toward the wall. She glances at me when we walk in, but to my relief, her eyes slide right over me and land back on the papers she's been leafing through. I don't know what I expect—I guess that she'll stand up, point at me, and scream, *Female! Female with a sock!*

"Yes, Tyler?"

"Ms. H., this is Nat Rodgers. He's new. Dr. Papadopoulos said I should show him around."

She looks up from the stack of paper. "First day?"

I nod. She swivels toward her computer monitor and starts clacking away at the keyboard with long red talons. A brass plaque on her desk reads *Ms. Honaker.* I stand there, waiting, painfully aware of my hands hanging at my sides but afraid to move them for fear of girly gestures.

"Nat—is that short for Nathan?"

Oh, God, *is* it short for Nathan? Darcy's little hacker cousin didn't give me much information. Then again, who names their kid *Nat*? Could it be short for something else? Nathaniel, maybe? Why didn't we cover this? Why, why, why?

"Uhh . . ."

"Oh! Here you are. Nat Rodgers. Just Nat. Okay . . ." She jabs at a few more keys, studies the screen. "Uh-*huh*. Very interesting."

My mouth feels so dry I'm not even sure I can speak.

"You just appeared"—she frowns at me over her glasses—"out of nowhere. We normally don't even take students mid-semester."

"It's hardly mid-semester," Tyler says. "Midterms aren't for another few weeks."

God bless the little POKSI; he's sticking up for me.

"Okay, well, let's get you settled, then. Fall semester started three weeks ago. It won't be easy, trying to catch up, and you're a junior, so you'll have to buckle down."

74

She takes her glasses off and uncoils from her chair. In one hand she cradles a huge coffee cup with the words *Born to Party. Forced to Work*. She uses it to gesture at a large, imposing oak door down the hall. "That's the headmaster's office, Dr. Papadopoulos. He likes to meet all the new boys, so we'll start there."

Tyler and I follow her. I notice she has on these beautiful Prada sling-backs in candy apple red. "Cute shoes."

She looks at me over her shoulder, an incredulous expression on her face. "I'm sorry?"

Cute shoes?!! Am I completely brain-dead? What sort of boy meets the school secretary and compliments her pumps? Tyler's behind me, so I can't see how he's taking this, but probably even he knows this isn't normal.

"I mean, they look new."

Ms. Honaker's eyebrows are still akimbo, but she accepts the compliment. "They are, actually. And thank you." Under her breath she adds, "That's a new one."

After a perfunctory knock on the oak door, she swings it open, saying, "Dr. Papadopoulos? We've got a new student here. Nat, this is the headmaster."

I peer around Ms. Honaker at the somber, tastefully furnished office and the man inside. Only his back is visible, but I can see a tall, powerfully built man with the confident, wide-legged stance of a football coach. His hands rest in the pockets of his charcoal gray suit while he stares out the window. He turns his head slightly but doesn't really look at us. "Hello. Welcome to Underwood. Ms. Honaker will take care of you, I'm sure."

"Hi, Dr. Papadopoulos," Tyler says. "I'm showing him around."

"Excellent, excellent."

With that, Ms. Honaker shuts the door and bustles back the way we came. Fine by me. The last thing I want is a lot of questions from Dr. Unpronounceable. I'm still pretty freaked out by my "cute shoes" slipup. If I expect to pull this off, I have to get into character and stay there.

Tyler leads me brusquely down the grand stone steps of the main building, back out into the parking lot. It's still early—my watch says seven forty—but there are quite a few students hanging around in groups, some of them cradling coffee in paper cups, all of them looking crisp and well pressed in their uniforms. I can feel their curious glances, but I'm afraid to make eye contact with anyone. If I see the slightest hint of suspicion in their faces it will totally psyche me out, so I keep my eyes mostly on the ground.

"That was the Hammond House we were just in," Tyler says brightly. "Most of the classes are in there. We'll stop by your car and get your bags, then I'll take you to your dorm and you can change into your uniform."

"Cool," I say. "Where do I get my uniform?"

He looks at me. "You mean you don't have one?"

"Uh, no. Should I?" *Scheisse!*

"Well, yeah. Most people buy them before their first day."

Triple *scheisse!* "I . . . didn't know that."

"They are *required*, you know." He stops walking, scrunches up his brow at me. "If you don't mind me asking, what's your story?"

"Wh-what do you mean?" Oh, God, this is it! He's totally onto me.

"Why are you starting school so late?"

"Oh! That. My family moved here sort of spur-of-the-moment. Dad got a new job. They heard Underwood's a lot better than Mountain View High, so . . ."

"Yeah, Mountain View's pretty scuzzy. You're more likely to get an STD there than an education." He snorts at his own joke.

I open my mouth to protest, close it just in time.

His brow furrows again. "But you can't just enroll on the spur-of-the-moment. You have to apply here way in advance."

"Oh. Yeah." I knew that! Why didn't I prepare for this? I should have a thorough explanation ready, and here I am making it up on the fly. "What I meant was I applied because we thought we'd move here and I got in, but then we thought Dad didn't get the job so we didn't move here and then at the last minute he *did* get it, so here I am." I spread my hands out like *ta-dah*! Christ, I'm sweating like a pig.

"Uh-huh."

"So anyway, about the uniform . . ."

"Right. The uniform." He looks me up and down. "You're about my size. I've got a couple extras if you want to borrow one for now."

I'm so relieved I clutch at his blazer in delight. "Really? You'd do that for me?"

A couple guys walking past do a double take and Tyler looks alarmed. He wriggles out of my grasp. "No biggie."

"Thank you!" I can see from the strange looks I'm getting that I'm standing out, so I quickly sling my thumbs through my belt loops, slouch, and try to look manly. "That'd be awesome."

●●●●●●●●●●●●●●●●●●●●●

Chapter Seven

●●●●●●●●●●●●●●●●●●●●●

$\mathcal{W}$e stop by the Buick and grab my duffel bag, then head down a footpath that leads from the parking lot to a four-story brick building covered in ivy. Darcy was right: It's a stunning campus. The rolling lawns are expansive seas of green spreading out in every direction.

"Here are the dorms." We've reached the brick building. "Each floor is for a different class. You're a junior, so you'll be on the third floor."

"Okay. Great!" A quick glance from him reminds me to back off on the enthusiasm. "I mean, cool."

"Let's see . . . who do they have you rooming with?" He pulls a piece of paper from his pocket and squints at it. "Oh, yeah, Emilio. He'll be bummed. Nobody with a single wants a roommate."

"Roommate?" Of course I'll have a roommate! Why didn't I think of that? Oh, God, how am I going to change my clothes? Am I really going to sleep next to a guy I've never even met? How weird is that? I can feel panic rising in me, a claustrophobic terror. "I thought I might room alone. Is that possible?"

Tyler guffaws. "Nobody gets their own room. Emilio's roommate transferred to Exeter at the last minute; that's the only reason he's on his own." Tyler yanks open the heavy door and leads me up a drafty cement stairwell, glancing over his shoulder. "Man, you look kind of sick. You okay?"

"Me?" It comes out as a squeak; I clear my throat. "Fine."

By now we've reached the third floor. Tyler leans against the metal bar, the door swings open, and we step into the hallway. The cold, echoing stairwell vanishes behind us and we're engulfed in chaos: doors slamming, guys laughing, people shouting. A guy in an Underwood blazer, socks, and no pants uses a plastic foosball bat to swat a crumpled ball of paper down the hall at his friend. The ball whizzes over everyone's heads and tags me on the cheek.

"Two points!" the batter cries.

"The junior floor," Tyler announces. "The dorms are a little hectic in the morning. I always get up at six to avoid the traffic."

I have to step back as a skinny, dark-haired, dripping wet guy wearing nothing but a towel almost runs me over.

"I can see why," I mumble.

As we make our way down the hall there's a stream of guys passing in and out of a room on our left. As we get closer and the door opens I can hear a cacophony of flushing toilets and showers; a cloud of steamy wet air escapes into the hall. The smell of cologne, toothpaste, shampoo, and other, earthier scents assault my nostrils. I make the mistake of turning to look and see a long line of guys in various states of undress doing their thing at the urinals.

Oh, God. Urinals. That's something else I'm not prepared for.

"It's not always this noisy," Tyler says as a guy on a skateboard whizzes past belting out some rap song at the top of his lungs, "but I recommend studying in the library. Okay, let's see . . . here's your room."

Tyler knocks twice and after a moment the door opens. There, standing before me, is a half-naked guy so gorgeous I do a double take. He's got dark, liquid eyes, close-cropped black hair, and smooth brown skin. His bare torso ripples with muscles: sculpted shoulders, well-defined pecs, and washboard abs. He's perfectly cut without veering into scary bodybuilder bulk. My attention jerks back to his eyes, which take me in warily.

"Hi." I can feel everything in me shifting into flirt mode. My hip automatically juts out to one side and the word comes out soft and fluttery.

Tyler and the guy at the door both look at me like I've just farted.

"I mean yo, what's up?"

Yo?

!!

"Uh, Emilio, this is your new roommate, Nat." Tyler looks apologetic.

"Roommate? Oh, *man* . . ."

"I know." Tyler holds up a hand. "It sucks, but you're the only junior with a single."

"Why didn't anyone give me a heads-up?" Emilio lets us into the room, which is small and sparsely furnished. There are two beds against the far wall, each one beneath a tall, wavy-paned window with curlicues of ivy peeking around the edges. One of the beds is unmade, so I toss my duffel bag onto the other.

"Last-minute thing, I guess," Tyler says. "He just kind of showed up."

Emilio grudgingly holds out a hand. "Sorry, man. Emilio Cruz. I'm not trying to be a jerk. I just like my privacy."

I shake his hand. His fingers are warm, his grip firm, and I have to fight the irrational impulse to pull him to me. "I understand. Don't mind me. I'll try to stay out of your way."

Tyler looks at his watch. "We better get you into uniform. Class starts in fifteen minutes."

"Oh, yeah, okay." I look back at Emilio, who's buttoning his shirt now. "Nice meeting you." The second it's out of my mouth I know it's geekily formal and wish I could take it back.

Emilio smiles with half his mouth. "Uh-huh."

I follow Tyler out, catching one last quick look at Emilio before the door swings shut. God, he's amazing. Why do I never meet boys like that when I'm a girl? The thought of living in close proximity to such a fine specimen fills me with equal parts horror and giddiness. I remind myself I'm on a mission here, not trolling for phone numbers. Any interest I have in Underwood boys must be purely professional.

Still, the image of a shirtless Emilio is burned into my brain.

Tyler's room is a few doors down. As we enter, the skinniest, palest boy I've ever seen stands buck-ass naked, one leg up on the bed, running a towel back and forth between his legs like dental floss.

I start to scream, then quickly cup a hand over my mouth.

Tyler looks at me like I'm crazy. "What's wrong now?"

I force myself to look at the floor. "Nothing. Just a cramp. I'll be fine."

Tyler gestures with one hand at the naked guy before heading straight for the closet. "My roommate, Max. Max, this is the new guy, Nat."

Max swings the towel around his neck and salutes. "Top of the morning to you!"

"Yeah," I say, still flustered.

"Okay, try this on." Tyler hands me a neatly pressed uniform on a hanger. "Hurry up! I can't be late for class."

Max, thank God, is pulling on a pair of tighty whiteys, so at least I don't have to concentrate on not looking at him. That's when it sinks in, though: Tyler expects me to change into his uniform. Here. In front of them.

I take the hanger from him, my mind reeling. "Uh, okay . . ."

He looks at his watch again. "Really, you have to hurry. I've got a quiz first period."

"See, the thing is . . ." I trail off. *The thing is* what? *The thing is you really can't see me naked because I've got two sports bras on and under that are small but nonetheless incriminating boobs*? "Mind if I change in the closet?"

Tyler and Max both stare at me, surprised.

"Why?" Tyler asks.

"Because I have . . . birthmarks!" I improvise.

"Birthmarks?" Max echoes.

"Yeah, birthmarks. Really weird ones. Hideous deformities—I don't want to talk about it." I dart to the closet.

"There's not much room in there," Tyler says doubtfully.

"I'll be fine." I quickly shut myself into the cramped, dark

84

space and, sweating profusely, change into Tyler's uniform. I stumble over his shoes a couple times but manage to get undressed and then dressed again without serious injury. I hurry back into the room, tucking in the shirt.

"You forgot the tie," Max says primly.

"Oh, yeah." I reach for the tie on the hanger, then realize I've no idea how to tie one. "Either of you guys know how to . . . ?"

"You never wore a tie before?" Tyler asks, incredulous.

"I'm just not that good at, you know, tying it."

Max sighs dramatically and crosses the room in his underwear and tube socks. His pale, fluffy hair makes him resemble a human Q-tip. He takes the tie from me and loops it around my neck with nimble fingers, lips pursed in disapproval. It's the closest I've ever been to a nearly naked male, and I have to say it's not at all how I imagined it.

"Didn't you have a uniform at your old school?" Tyler asks.

"Sure," I say. "I just never got good at the tie, I guess."

"Did Mommy do it for you?" Max finishes his work by tightening the knot around my neck.

"Jeez," I protest. "Mind if I breathe?"

"Como on!" Tyler hustles me toward the door. "We've got to go. If I miss points on this quiz my day will be ruined."

I mumble a quick thanks to Max and follow Tyler out.

"See you at lunch!" Max calls just before the door slams.

I hurry after Tyler, who is practically running now.

"We'll go through the courtyard," he says. "That way I can give you a quick rundown of the social landscape before first period. Here's your schedule."

I take the printout from him. "The social landscape?"

"Yeah—you know. Who's who, what's what."

I scramble down the footpath after him, back toward the big, Gothic building the headmaster's office is in. I can't help gazing up at it again in wonder. It really is impressive, with its spires and towers and huge, beautiful windows.

"This is where everyone hangs out," Tyler says.

I don't really see anyone around and I'm about to ask what he's talking about when we turn a corner and find ourselves at the edge of a beautiful cobblestone courtyard. At its center is a quaint stone fountain spewing plumes of froth. The space is filled with guys in uniform; some sit at picnic tables or benches, some stand around in tight circles, still others lounge at the edge of the fountain, their faces turned up to the sun.

Tyler looks at me. "So here goes your five-minute tour of the social strata. Ready?"

"Ready."

"Over there you've got your more-organic-than-thou types." He nods at a group of skinny guys draped on the fire escape that snakes up the building. "Vegans, animal rights activists, stewards of the earth. They're always on the administration about the meal options, and no matter what we're discussing in class they'll find a way to drag in the melting polar ice caps."

"Roger that," I say. "Earth stewards, two o'clock."

"Here you've got your frustrated metal heads." He nods at a table covered in sullen-looking guys with hair that hangs into their eyes. "In the real world they'd have mass hair and piercings, but Underwood precludes that particular form of personal expression, so they're stuck with greasy bangs. After school they're smoking in the woods, if you need them. They can get you any drug for a small handling fee, but you should give them at least one week advance notice."

"I'll keep that in mind," I say.

"To our left you'll see the future Republican power brokers. They already have investment portfolios that would make Donald Trump proud."

I nod, taking in the picnic table filled with clean-cut guys all glued to laptops and BlackBerrys.

I hear a sharp bark of laughter across the courtyard and turn to see Josh, the guy Chloe's into, standing on the edge of the fountain tossing a Frisbee to someone. "What about those guys?"

"Good eye. Around the fountain's prime real estate." Tyler nods sagely. "They're upper crust. Mostly athletes—

water polo players, soccer, tennis. We don't have a football team, so we're spared that brutal form of idolatry, but we manage to produce other kinds of jocks."

"Is that guy a jock?" I nod at Josh. I figure I better have some insights for Chloe when I see her tonight or she'll be pissed.

"Water polo captain, but the season hasn't started yet. That means he's doing the drama thing for now."

"Is he nice?"

Tyler makes a face. "Nice?"

"I mean, you know, cool?"

Tyler slaps me on the back. "Let me put it this way: Don't try engaging Josh Mayer in a friendly chat. He's a god. No mingling with us mortals."

I can't help bristling slightly. Tyler's POKSI status is already firmly established, at least in my mind. Okay, so he's a clever guy, I'll give him that, but he's not what you'd call popular. Now he's lumping me in with his tribe! That's just insulting. I've never been Little Miss Homecoming Queen, but I've always been popular. Yeah, sure, as a guy I might seem less than über-macho and that could hinder my hip-factor, but I can't spend this week clinging to the fringe, or I'll never get the answers I need. My article's not called "A Girls' Guide to Geeks," after all. If I'm going to get the 411 on the guys worth knowing, I've got to get in with them right away. When it comes to cliques, you have to make headway with the right crowd your first day or the stigma of being seen with losers will hinder you.

I turn my attention back to the fountain and see that Josh has just caught the Frisbee and is about to toss it again. He really is gorgeous; perfectly mussed hair, beautiful dark blue eyes. His skin is a delicate peaches-'n'-cream, rosy along the rims of his cheekbones in the cool morning air. If it weren't for his strong, athletic build and impressive height he might almost be too pretty. I can see why Chloe's into him.

I decide it must be fate when the breeze derails the Frisbee Josh just threw and sends it in my direction. Okay, only vaguely in my direction; I have to leap for it, but I manage to intercept it, albeit clumsily.

Tyler looks horrified. "Just toss it back," he orders out of the side of his mouth.

"Why? I'm going to introduce myself."

"Not a good idea."

"Oh, come on," I say. "What's the harm?"

Tyler shakes his head, staring at the ground. "I've got to review for that history quiz. Toss it back and I'll take you to your first class."

"You go ahead. I'm going to network." Ignoring his terrified expression, I grip the Frisbee and make my way over to Josh. Is it my imagination, or has a hush suddenly come over the courtyard? What's the big deal? I'm just going to talk to the guy.

"Hi." I present Josh with the Frisbee and smile my friendliest smile. "How's it going? I'm new here."

Josh takes the proffered Frisbee, but eyes it suspiciously. "Uh-huh. I can see that."

"I hear you're an actor. And water polo captain too. Impressive."

Josh shoots a look at his friends: *Can you believe this guy?* I can feel myself starting to blush, but there's no way to terminate the conversation gracefully now that I'm committed, so I stick out a hand. "I'm Nat."

Josh grins. "Nat. The name fits."

"Thanks."

"An annoying insect who doesn't know when it's not wanted."

Josh's friends burst into raucous laughter just as the chimes signal the start of first period.

Okay, then. That went well.

●●●●●●●●●●●●●●●●●●
Chapter Eight
●●●●●●●●●●●●●●●●●●

*B*y the end of third period I have to pee so badly, I swear my bladder's swollen to five times its natural size; it's squeezing all my other internal organs into remote corners of my body like a fat lady on a crowded subway. I just can't face the urinals! They're way too terrifying. The smell, the exposed bits, the shame. Isn't using a stall the same as announcing I have to take a dump? How completely embarrassing! Yet I can hardly line up with the others and whip out my sock.

After several agonizing hours of holding it, though, I can't handle another second. I scuttle to the bathroom with my knees together. Despite my urgent need to relieve myself, I pause at the door, heart pounding. A couple guys walk by covertly fishing cigarettes from their blazer pockets; when they see me standing there gazing at the door, their laughter stops abruptly and they exchange a look.

Obviously I can't hesitate another second or I'll arouse suspicion. I take a deep breath and shove. I guess I'm a bit too aggressive about it, because I hear the door thwack against something solid. Cringing, I step inside and see Emilio, my gorgeous roommate, pressing the heel of his right hand against his eyebrow.

"Scheisse!" I cry, alarmed. "I'm so sorry!"

He shakes his head like someone waking from a dream. "Whoa. Wasn't expecting the door to attack. Did you say *'scheisse'*?" When he pulls his hand away I can see blood on his forehead.

"Oh no, you're bleeding!"

He examines his face in the mirror, but offers no comment. I rush to the sink, yank a paper towel from the dispenser, and wet it. I suspect this isn't very guy-like, but I hand it to him anyway, stopping myself from actually dabbing at the wound.

He takes the damp towel from me with a skeptical expression. "Uh, thanks."

I hear the sound of streaming liquid to my left and almost jump when I see two guys peeing at the urinals. Aaagh! The smell! The sordid publicness of it all!

"You okay?" Emilio asks, looking amused.

"Yeah!"

I say it too loudly and one of the guys at the urinals glances over his shoulder, annoyed. I can't imagine the concentration it must take to pee in public, especially standing up.

I turn my attention back to Emilio, who is watching me with an amused expression as he presses the paper towel to his forehead. "You sure you're okay? You look freaked out."

I nod and try for a casual shrug. "I'm going to use a stall."

His eyebrows arch in surprise. "Um, okay."

"Not that I have to—you know, pinch a loaf or anything—I just prefer privacy." Stop. Talking. Stop! Talking!

Emilio puts both hands up in the universal *not my business* gesture and backs out the door.

I want to die. I seriously want to die. I just said "pinch a loaf" to the cutest guy I've ever seen.

I scurry into one of the stalls, lock myself in, and frantically pull my pants down. I remember to grab the sock before it falls into the toilet, thank God. Not sure how I'd deal with that one. When at last I get to pee, the release is almost excruciating in its pleasure. I want to moan, but settle for a satisfied sigh.

The dining hall is, like everything else at Underwood, imposing and majestic. It has a vaulted ceiling, gleaming oak floors, and long, polished mahogany tables. The evening light pours in through the towering, skinny windows of the west wall, spilling into the room in buttery pools. It feels more like a church than a cafeteria.

This is the first time I've been in here, since I skipped lunch. After my disastrous attempt to make friends with Josh this morning in the courtyard and my equally mortifying run-in with Emilio in the bathroom, I spent the forty-minute break between fourth and fifth period eating vending machine chips and a Snickers bar in my car, talking to Darcy on the phone, lying down in the backseat so no one would see me there and get suspicious.

I've made it through the day without blowing my cover, though, and for that I'm incredibly grateful. It's been a lot more challenging than I imagined—I can't remember the last time I felt this out of my element. I'm in a completely foreign culture with its own language and customs, yet I'm only fifteen minutes from home.

Luckily, classes pose no threat since they're lecture style. I don't have to say a single word; so long as I look marginally engaged, the teachers seem satisfied. I've gotten past the initial terror of thinking each new person I encounter will take one look at me and yell, "But she's a *girl*!" At the most basic level I'm obviously passing. Still, the subtler aspects of guyness elude me. The way they move, cocksure and easy. The way they interact with each other—so understated and terse they're practically talking in code. I've gone to school with guys, hung out with them my whole life, and yet somehow I never noticed just how different they really are. It's not like I'm the femmiest girl in town, yet now that I'm trying to camouflage my girly qualities I see just how pronounced those aspects of my personality really are.

Everything I do naturally earns me funny looks here. I don't catch myself until just a second too late, but by then it's impossible to remedy. When the drama teacher made a joke, my laugh came out too shrill and everyone turned to stare. Walking across campus between classes, I didn't notice I was swinging my hips until I saw the raised eyebrows and double takes. In math class, out of sheer boredom, I started winding a lock of hair around my finger, but stopped when the guy next to me snorted. It's like all my instincts backfire here. I never imagined just how deeply ingrained my own girlyness is, or how suspect that girlyness makes me in a man's world.

I sit in the corner of the dining hall nibbling my mashed potatoes, peas, and sliced turkey breast. It's not exactly restaurant quality, but it's better than your average high school cafeteria fare. I'm hungry, but the nervousness that's turned my stomach into a war zone makes me wary of eating too much too quickly. My whole body is bone tired; being someone you're not all day takes way more energy than you'd think. I can't wait to see Chloe and Darcy tonight when they come to campus for rehearsal. The thought of being able to let down my guard with people who know me sounds like heaven.

I watch as Josh and his friends come in, pile their plates high with food, and sit at a table in the center of the room. They move with the easy, loose-limbed assurance of athletes. They sit with their knees splayed, talking and laughing so loudly that their voices ricochet off the high ceilings, punctuated now and then with the slap of a high five. What's it like to have that much confidence? How does it feel, knowing you own the world? More importantly, how will I ever get guys like them to answer my questions? I can't reach them as a girl because then I'm either the mark or the enemy, but as nerd-boy I'm no closer to knowing their secrets.

A couple tables away, sitting by himself, I spot Emilio. He gazes out the window, a faraway look in his eyes. The evening light shines on his face as he chews slowly, lost in thought. With a blink he snaps back from his reverie and turns his head. I realize with a start that he's staring directly at me. My ears burn as I look away.

"How's it going?" Tyler sits down beside me, and I can't help smiling. I might not be popular here at Underwood, but at least I'm not a complete social leper.

"Okay, I guess."

Max and a very short guy with shaggy dark hair sit down opposite us.

Tyler says, "You met my roommate, Max, this morning."

I nod in acknowledgment, trying not to recall the naked

butt-flossing mid-chew. Max salutes again. What's the deal with that? He's like a weird little wind-up soldier.

Tyler gestures at the short guy. "This is Earl. He's a genius."

"Oh, yeah?" I grin, careful to keep my tone relatively unimpressed. I'm learning to tamp down my natural exuberance. In Boyland, enthusiasm is suspect. "That must be cool—being a genius, I mean."

"Technically, his statement is accurate, though I don't go around announcing it. My IQ is one eighty-one on the Wechsler Scale, which is considered by most to be within the genius realm." He speaks in a mumbling monotone, and I have to lean closer to hear him. "Of course, some people say all IQ tests contain ranking fallacies and cultural biases, though my strongest area of cognition is in calculating number sequences that are impossible to imbue with gender or ethnic partiality—"

"He never knows when to shut up," Tyler interrupts, spearing a piece of meat and shoveling it into his mouth.

I'm thrown by Tyler's bluntness. Girls hardly ever say mean shit like that to someone's face! Unless they're Chloe, that is. A strangled chortle escapes before I can stop it. Everyone within earshot glances over, looking annoyed. I offer an apologetic little smile and concentrate on my mashed potatoes. Great! Now even the weirdos think I'm weird.

The anxiety that's been slowly burning at the back of my

brain all day starts to gain momentum. Sure, I'm behind enemy lines, but what good is that unless I can get some real answers to my seven questions? I'm like a spy who manages to infiltrate a terrorist cell but never learns anything because she doesn't speak the language. So far I've got exactly nothing to bring back to the girls of the world who are counting on me and my insights.

I cast a wistful eye over Josh's table again; he and his friends are cracking up about something. One of them catches me staring and makes a face—not a friendly, come-on-over-and-hang-out face, but a you're-such-a-retard-you-don't-even-deserve-to-look-at-us face. That makes the other guys laugh still harder. God, I'm a full-on certified loser! How am I going to undo this reputational damage fast enough to get in with those guys? It's impossible. They've decided I'm sub-cool, so that's what I am.

I look around at Tyler, Max, and Earl, who are talking about the improved graphics on some video game. No doubt about it: I've landed smack in the middle of Dweebville. Nobody in this dining hall looks quite so gangly or awkward as these three. Still, they were nice enough to sit with me. They're kind of cool in their own way. Well, okay, not cool-cool, but sweet, sort of. Why not start my research here? Granted, these guys aren't the ones most girls are dying to know about, but they are *guys*, right? Maybe there are certain qualities all males have in common, no matter where they are in the social hierarchy. Anyway, how are readers going to know what ilk of boy I got my answers from? It's not like I'll include pictures.

"So, I was wondering," I say, interrupting their enthusiastic discussion of first person shooter graphics. "Have any of you ever told a girl you'd call her and then just blown her off?"

The silence that ensues is deafening, even in the noisy dining hall.

"Let's just say, hypothetically"—my cheeks burn as they all stare at me—"if you met a girl and you said you were going to call her but then you didn't, what might be the reason for that?"

"Wait, what's the question?" Tyler glances at his friends like maybe he's missing the joke, but they just stare at me blank-faced.

"If you said you'd call her and you didn't, why didn't you? She'd totally be expecting you to, or at least text or e-mail or whatever, and then when you don't do *anything*, when you just disappear without a trace, she's like, God, what happened? I mean, I can imagine that, anyway."

"What are you talking about?" Tyler says finally. "What girl?"

I sigh. "Let's back up. Have any of you ever told a girl you'd call her?"

They glance at one another, then shake their heads in unison.

"None of you have ever said to a girl, 'I'll call you'? Are you *serious*?" I'm not trying to be mean, but God, this is sad. These are seventeen-year-old red-blooded males we're talking about, not monks!

"I don't know if you noticed," Max says defensively, "but there aren't any girls at Underwood. You want us to ask out Ms. Honaker?"

Tyler and Earl snort.

I frown at them. "You're not prisoners here, right? Don't you ever get out and meet chicks?"

Tyler cuts his eyes at Josh's table. "Girls like those kind of guys. They're not into us."

"Some do, sure, but not all of them." Admittedly, that was my main objection to getting answers from these odd-ball new friends of mine—girls *aren't* interested in what they think. Now, though, I find myself suddenly resisting that basic truth. I mean, they might not be super-sexy, but they're the only ones who befriended me here, and that's got to count for something. Surely there are girls somewhere in the world who would find them attractive. "Plenty of girls would dig you if you put yourselves out there more. Haven't you heard of geek-chic? Look at Michael Cera!"

"Do *you* have a girlfriend?" Earl asks.

Hmm . . . that's not a bad idea, actually. Maybe I can use this. "Yeah. I mean, we're not engaged or anything, but I see this girl on occasion. We're kind of into each other. She's the one who was asking me why guys say they're going to call and then just don't. I'm like, 'I don't know, babe.' 'Cause you know, if I say I'm going to call, that's what I do. I call."

"Uh-huh." Tyler's looking at me like he can't figure me out. Actually, they all are.

I press on. "Another thing she was asking me about is why guys are so different around their friends. Like alone with a girl they're one way, and then hanging with their friends, they're a totally different person. We are, I mean. Some guys, anyway. You know what I'm saying?"

Silence.

"Anyway, that's what she says. I don't know why she's all worried about it. Chicks!"

Max turns to Earl. "The thing about Blood Frontier is it doesn't work as well on Linux."

"I know," Earl agrees. "That's my complaint too. I'm not sure if that's because it's open source software or if the problem runs deeper than that."

Wow. I'm really making some headway here. Before you know it I'll be a full-fledged expert. I'll have to change the focus of my article slightly, but that's okay. I'm sure readers don't care much about the inner workings of male behavior. I'm sure they'd much rather read about the minutia of Blood Frontier.

I choke down another few bites of dinner, say good-bye to the gamer gang, and head for the door. This is not what I pictured at all. Sure, I'm inside Underwood, but what good does that do me if I can't get inside their heads?

As I step outside the dining hall the crisp fall air feels good. I take a deep breath and look out over the majestic lawn to where the sun sparkles on the ocean like sequins scattered across swaths of blue silk. It really is an unbelievably romantic setting, with its ivy-covered towers, Gothic spires, and panoramic views of the sea; leave it to me to land myself in a place like this, surrounded by hot guys, yet be unable to do anything about it.

"How'd the first day go?"

I turn to see Emilio just behind me, hands in his pockets. His dark eyes rest on my face for a moment before moving past me to the ocean view.

"Not bad," I say, but my tone does nothing to disguise my dejected mood.

"First days are the hardest," he says.

I start to answer, but he's already turned and is striding away. I watch him until he disappears down the footpath, his silhouette melting into the shadows of the shrubbery.

Chapter Nine

I find a bench at the far edge of campus and sit down, relieved to be alone and unobserved at last. Even though I just talked to Darcy at lunch, I feel an almost overwhelming urge to hear her voice again. Time at Underwood moves so slowly; it seems like days have passed since I huddled in the Buick and whispered news of my morning to her. I'm so glad she and Chloe will be here tonight for rehearsal. I take out my cell and dial Darcy's number.

She answers immediately. "How did it go? Tell me everything!"

I smile. It's such a girl thing to say: *Tell me everything.* I already miss that—the greedy urge to devour the details of others' lives.

"Being here is such a trip."

"And . . . ?" she prompts, impatient. "Come on! I want details."

I feel suddenly overwhelmed by the prospect of explaining my afternoon. "I'll fill you in later tonight. How's everything there?"

"I've been putting out fires every five minutes. I expect a bronze best friend plaque at the end of all this. Actually, make it solid gold—I deserve it."

I bite my lip, suddenly worried. "What kind of fires?"

"You know, just covering—telling teachers you're sick, stuff like that. I ran into your mom downtown and she was like, *I thought you and Natalie were working on a school project?*"

I wince. "What did you say?"

"I went into this detailed explanation about how you were back at my place cutting up newspaper for a papier-mâché model of the central nervous system. She was like *I thought it was a history project* so I made something up about a cross-discipline history-biology research thingy."

"You think she bought it?" I'm imagining the scene: my mother's baffled face, Darcy talking a mile a minute.

"My explanation was so convoluted—who would go to the trouble of making up something that confusing? So yeah, I guess she took my word for it."

"Thank God." My mom's pretty chill—or oblivious, depending on how you look at it. She trusts me and doesn't pry, usually. Then again, I've never pulled a stunt like this before, so I can't be totally sure her usual cluelessness will hold all week.

"Chloe's like yanking the phone from me. She's dying to talk to you."

"How sweet . . ." I say, touched.

"Not really. She wants to know if Josh likes her."

I snort. "Figures. Listen, I'm going to sneak into the theater tonight and meet you after rehearsal, okay? Is there someplace over there that's private?"

"There's a funky little prop closet just down the hall from the greenroom. Want to meet us there? We should be done before ten."

"What about Summer, though? Any chance she'll walk in on us?"

She scoffs. "Are you kidding? Like that prima donna would get anywhere near a dusty old storage room. Besides, she always leaves right when rehearsal's over. I think she gets a ride from her sister or something."

"Cool. See you then." I put my phone back in my pocket and look west again. The sky has gone from mauve to neon pink as the sun moves in slow motion toward the sea. The clouds smeared along the horizon are a luminous peach.

I may not be in like Flynn with the coolest Underwoodies, but I'm here, right? My disguise is working and I'm in their midst—I should be proud of myself for getting this far. I do need to make the most of every minute, though. Hanging out with Tyler and company doesn't seem very promising. Maybe just spying on the ruling class will provide me with some answers. Josh is in the play, so apparently sex gods do theater around here; that means I can skulk in the shadows while I wait for Chloe and Darcy to be done, maybe learn a little more about what Josh and his brethren are really made of.

Walking back across campus I run into a cluster of the stringy-haired guys Tyler referred to as frustrated metal heads. They're making their way toward the woods, lighting up cigarettes with quick, furtive glances over their shoulders. I ask them where the theater is and they flick their long bangs in the direction of the Hammond House. I pass some guys playing soccer in the tawny light and a couple of scrawny kids hunched over a chessboard at a picnic table, looking like little old men.

I'm not prepared for the Underwood theater; not by a long shot. As I make my way inside, I actually catch my breath in surprise. Luckily, nobody's in there yet, so I'm free to check it out unobserved. It's one of the most unbelievable venues I've ever seen. There are at least five hundred red velvet seats, including two balconies—both a dress and an upper circle. The arched ceiling is a creamy white carved with swirling designs like a wedding cake. Paneled walls line the front of the house, complete with art deco sconces shedding fans of gold. The stage is amazing: It's framed by a proscenium arch elaborately painted with gods and goddesses cavorting through muted, jewel-toned gardens. Merlot-colored curtains are drawn, revealing a set that's nearly done. A crystal chandelier casts a pool of lemony light on the gleaming hardwood stage, and elegant Victorian furniture fills out the space.

Wow. What I wouldn't give to act on a stage like that! The auditorium at our high school looks like a shoebox compared to this. I can feel my old drama instincts kicking in: the empty stage beckons. I check my cell phone to see what time it is. Darcy said rehearsal starts at seven. It's only six forty. I'll just stand up there, feel the space, remember what it's like, then scurry back to the shadows before anyone arrives.

I make my way quietly up the stage left steps. The house lights are on, so it's not like being onstage during a show—there's no blinding hot flood turning everything before me into a sea of black—but still, I can feel it. The magic. I remember the long hours I spent rehearsing for this play, learning the part of Cecily, walking through the blocking in my room at night since I didn't get to rehearse it very often with the cast. I knew that role inside and out. It was such a drag that I never got to play it even once. Usually our drama teacher gives the understudy one show, but Summer pitched a fit when he suggested it, stomped her little D&G-clad foot like a toddler, so he caved. Jerk.

I cross down stage right, imagining the whisper of my silk skirts against the floor. I can see myself playing that first scene, set in the garden of Uncle Jack's manor house. My governess, Miss Prism, is trying to persuade me to sit down and attend to my lessons. "But I don't like German. It isn't at all a becoming language. I know perfectly well that I look quite plain after my German lesson."

"Summer? Is that you?"

I whip around to see Emilio emerging from the wings. I almost scream, but stop myself just in time.

"Oh, hey. It's you." His brow furrows. "I thought I heard Summer in here rehearsing."

I look around. "No. I heard someone too, though. A girl. Not me. I didn't say anything. Maybe she's um . . . in the greenroom."

"Okay. I'll look." He doesn't move, though. "What are you doing here? You act?"

"No! Not really. I just saw the stage and thought I'd check it out."

He nods at the gorgeous stage. "Pretty cool, huh?"

"Oh my God!" I gush. "It's the most spectacular theater I've ever seen! It's like so huge and so incredibly . . ."

He gives me a funny look, and I trail off. Too much enthusiasm again. Got to get a handle on that.

I wipe the smile off my face and try for nonchalance. "Anyway, I heard you guys are doing a play. You in it?"

"Yeah."

"What role?" I ask, wondering why Darcy and Chloe never mentioned him.

"Algernon."

"You're one of the leads!" I say. "That's great."

He looks at his shoes shyly. God, he's adorable. "So you know the play?"

"I—yeah. Somewhat. Here and there. Might have seen it once."

"Yoo-hoo! Anybody here?" The sound of Summer's voice heading toward us sends my heart bumping around inside my rib cage like a trapped hummingbird.

"On the stage!" Emilio calls, turning back to face the wings. "I thought I heard you."

Scheisse! Summer can't see me here or I'm so completely screwed! I scurry into the wings stage right just as she enters stage left.

Behind me, I hear Emilio say, "Hi. You look great."

"Thanks. So do you."

"Uh, meet my new roommate—" Pause. Emilio's tone becomes puzzled, a little embarrassed. "He was right here."

But I'm nowhere to be seen, of course. I can't afford to be. I climb the ladder to the catwalk, where I hope to watch the rehearsal without being noticed. Luckily, it's the ideal setup for spying. The T-shaped metal walkway suspended above the stage is perfectly placed; I can see everything, but it's far enough above the stage to be draped in shadow, so anyone who might happen to glance up will still be oblivious to my presence. Score!

"Are you talking to imaginary friends?" Summer's flirtatious tone is cloyingly sweet. "Was that Bunbury?"

Oh, she's so clever, with her witty little reference to the script. I've always hated that about certain theater types—constantly working lines from the play into conversation, using them as inside jokes. It's like they don't have any witticisms of their own without ripping off some poor dead playwright. Summer's the epitome of that. From up here I can see the top of her head, shiny, golden hair spilling out in every direction. She's got the kind of hair that's maddeningly vibrant and versatile. One day she'll blow-dry it straight and silky smooth, the next she'll wear it in alluring, fairy tale princess ringlets. Today it's sort of in between: loose waves cascading over her shoulders. Now that I've chopped mine off I'm even less equipped to compete. Not that I have to. That's why I stopped auditioning, so I won't always be competing with her. God, I despise her.

"I was hoping you'd get here early." Summer takes a couple steps toward Emilio.

"Really?" He looks down at the stage. Oh, wow! Emilio's

shy. Look at him; even his scalp is blushing. He's completely irresistible. "You ready for tech week?"

Summer does her patented hair flip and moves closer. She's so after him! Last I checked she was dating Robbie Herbert. Skank!

"It's not that big of a deal. You just stand there while they adjust the lights. This show isn't very technically demanding anyway. It should be a breeze."

"It's really my first play." He's still staring at his shoes.

One more step, and she's practically in his lap. "So you've done, what? Film and TV before this?"

He chuckles. "No! I've never done anything."

"I don't believe it!" Her hand lands on his shoulder. Totally moving in for the kill. "That's impossible."

"Unless you count a Christmas pageant ten years ago. I was Shepherd Number Four."

She opens her mouth and laughs like it's the most hilarious thing any human being ever uttered. I mean, sure, it was cute, but she's overplaying it a bit, isn't she? God, do I laugh like that when I'm flirting? If so, somebody shoot me now.

When she finally catches her breath she squeezes his arm and leans in even closer. "Oh, you're so talented! You've got to pursue it. It would be criminal not to. I can totally introduce you to my agent. She's with William Morris? In LA? She'll get you jobs like that." She snaps her manicured fingers. "It's so hard to find good Latino actors."

Ew! Did she really just say that? I try to gauge Emilio's reaction, but whatever he's thinking doesn't show on his face.

Suddenly the doors at the front of the house burst open and a man's singsong voice calls out, "Where are my people? I need my people!"

I turn and watch as Mr. Pratt, the drama teacher, struts down the center aisle. His wild bleach blond hair looks even messier than it did this morning in class. He wears designer jeans, a cashmere sweater, and an impeccably cut sports coat—very chic. Behind him a host of others stream in: a harried-looking man toting lights, a fat twenty-ish guy with an enormous plastic soda cup, Ms. Honaker, Tyler, Earl, and Max. Finally, bringing up the rear I spot Josh and Chloe, followed by Darcy. *My* people! I want to clamber down the catwalk and hug my two best girls, but of course I stay where I am.

"Ms. Honaker," the blond man says in an imperious tone. "I trust we'll be in costume tomorrow night? You ladies will need time to adjust to those elaborate hats, you know."

"I'm used to them, Mr. Pratt," Summer calls from the stage. "I've done the show be—"

"Yes, we all know, darling. You've done the show before." His tone is catty. I like him! Anyone who talks to Summer like that is a friend of mine.

"I'm just saying . . ." Summer grumbles.

"Yes, you're 'just saying,' aren't you?" He folds his arms and squints at Summer and Emilio, who are still onstage. "What are you two doing up there? I hope you're not rehearsing behind my back!"

"No!" Emilio says. "We're just hanging out."

"Ah, the dreaded 'hanging out.' You're not flirting, I hope! Or God forbid anything else. It completely destroys onstage chemistry if you're groping each other in the wings."

I swear Emilio turns so red he looks like he might require medical attention.

Mr. Pratt gets down to business then, ordering everyone around. He spends lots of time talking to the fat guy with the mega-soda, the tired guy, and Earl—his crew. It's the first night of tech week, which means a lot of boring standing around for the actors. They gather onstage but don't get to run scenes all the way through the way they would at a normal rehearsal; instead they go from cue to cue, saying a line and then waiting endlessly while people run around changing gels and spiking set pieces. It's a total drag.

I have to say, though, observing it from this angle is kind of fascinating. Since there's so much downtime in between cues, I get to eavesdrop on the conversations that inevitably bubble up in the long pauses, even though Mr. Pratt keeps telling them in no uncertain terms to shut up.

Chloe's really working it with Josh. Of course I've seen

her in action before, but this is different. Usually I'm—well, there. As another girl, I mean. When you're part of a scene, it's a lot harder to observe it. Now I get to sit back and analyze her flirting style with perfect objectivity. Every single time Josh tries to engage her in conversation, she either ignores him or responds with the snarkiest retort possible. It's sort of shocking, actually. I can't believe I never noticed it before! She's incredibly bitchy. And yeah, okay, so bitchyness is sort of her style, even around Darcy and me. Here's the difference, though: With us, there's always an underlying affection and loyalty. With Josh, it's just . . . bitchy. Yet it has an almost magical effect on him. The more she abuses him, the more determined he becomes to win her over. Either he gets off on the thrill of the hunt or he's a masochist.

"You coming to my party Friday night?" Josh asks her as they wait for the lighting guy to adjust the upstage Fresnel.

"A party on opening night?" she sneers. "Isn't that bad luck or something?"

"Not if you're there," he says.

Now he's Prince Charmalot. I think of what a jerk he was to me today—well, Nat, anyway—and roll my eyes.

"I don't know." She examines her nails. "I might be busy."

"Come on! You've never been to my house before." He puts a hand on her elbow. "I can take you up to my room and show you my etchings."

114

Chloe makes a sound in her throat. "Cheesy!"

"See what you do to me? I'm forced to use really bad pickup lines."

She ignores this and studies her split ends with intense concentration. If I didn't know better, I'd seriously think she was giving him the brush-off. How does she manage that? Not to be unkind, but of the three of us, I always considered Chloe the least promising at acting. Now I see she's really quite convincing when she's writing her own script.

Tyler comes over and hands Chloe a shawl. "Ms. Honaker thought you might want this."

Chloe shoots him a withering glare. "Why?"

"Uh, because your costume has a—you know—"

"A *shawl*," she says, like she's addressing child, "it's called a shawl."

"Yeah. So she wants you to get used to it. As a prop."

She looks utterly disgusted. "It's a costume element, not a prop."

"I just meant—"

"Whatever, *manservant*! Here, I'll drape it over me. Does that make you happy?"

Josh laughs.

"It's n-not me," Tyler stammers, "Ms. Honaker. She wants—"

"Yeah. I got that," Chloe says in a tone that clearly says *You're dismissed.*

Okay, can I just say? My friend Chloe? Nowhere in sight. Her evil twin? Very much present. I mean really, what was that? When she's Cruella with Josh it doesn't bother me—the guy's been nothing but rude to me all day. But Tyler? He's smart and kind and obviously just trying to help. He's even cute if you really look at him! Those pretty gray eyes? The expressive eyebrows? And Chloe, my friend since the second grade, who deep down has a very big, very generous heart, has sweet little Tyler so freaked out he's stammering. Articulate, funny Tyler develops an instant speech impediment—that's how intimidating she is.

How's Chloe ever going to get with anyone but assholes like Josh if she behaves so bitchily? And if she gets screwed over by him, who can she possibly blame except herself?

Darcy's way on the other side of the spectrum. While Chloe treats every guy like something disgusting she's just scraped off the bottom of her shoe, Darcy treats them like the strangers her mom warned her about. Josh doesn't pay any attention to her, and she doesn't dare attempt to engage him in conversation. Tyler, though, seems kind of interested. He keeps making lame jokes and checking out her reaction with sideways glances.

"Hey, what if Lady Bracknell had pink hair?" Tyler suggests.

"We're getting Darcy a wig," snaps Ms. Honaker impatiently. "It should be here tomorrow."

Darcy's eyes dart from one face to another, but she says nothing.

"I know, but I'm just saying, it would be cool. This proper old lady with hot pink hair? Maybe we should set the whole thing in the eighties. Jack could be like a hair band dude, and Algernon could be a break-dancer."

This gets a tiny smile from Darcy. I totally expect her to join in with casting and costume ideas—she loves bad eighties everything—but she looks at the floor and stays silent.

Frankly, I'm mystified. I know for a fact that Chloe and Darcy are two of the coolest girls in existence. Yet who are they around guys—at least these ones? Chloe's PMS personified and Darcy . . . well, Darcy's not saying a word. She's been silent all night, except when Mr. Pratt orders her to say a line. My colorful, fearless friend has displayed the personality of a potato.

Why have I never really noticed this before? Sure, I know Chloe can be harsh and her flirting style's a bit acerbic. I know Darcy often gets shy around guys she doesn't know. That's part of why she's wasted so much time clinging to Rob, I guess; he's one of the few guys she feels comfortable around. But watching Chloe and Darcy tonight is so eye-opening. It's like seeing them for the first time.

This leads me to the scariest question of all: What am *I* like around guys? Both Chloe and Darcy have more relationship experience than I do. You'd think that would make them more comfortable, less likely to play head games. If they seem this unnatural—this unlike themselves—how must I seem?

Weird. I'm going to have to talk to them about this. Our rendezvous in the prop closet is suddenly more urgent than ever.

It seems like I've been waiting in this stuffy little room for hours. It's pitch-black, but I'm afraid to turn on the light because someone might notice. I'm sure being discovered in here all alone for no apparent reason will do wonders for my already firmly established reputation as freak of the month. Luckily there's a beanbag in the far corner, so I'm sitting here, cross-legged, reflecting on my very strange day.

Finally, at ten twenty, I get a text from Darcy: *Are you in the prop closet?*

I write back: *Yeah! Where are you?*

Coming in a minute. Trying to get C away from J. Arg!

Shaking my head, I write back: *No kidding . . .*

Five minutes later Darcy bursts in, followed by Chloe. The room explodes with light.

"What are you doing in the dark?" Chloe demands.

"I didn't want to get caught."

"Since when are you so paranoid?" she asks, picking her way around a plaster statue in her heels.

"Um, since I decided to go undercover at an all-boys prep school, maybe?"

Darcy comes right over and plops down beside me on the beanbag. I'm not usually super-demonstrative, but it's so great to see her again that I give her a hug.

"I missed you guys," I say. "Being a dude is weird."

Darcy's eyes go wide. "Is it incredible? It must be so fun!"

"Not at all!" I hang my head. "I'm a complete dweeb. It's embarrassing."

Chloe sits down on a nearby stool and brushes lint from her pants. "So you're finally getting in touch with your inner loser."

"Seriously!" I whine. "I'm like the social equivalent of herpes."

"Attractive metaphor." Chloe leans forward. "Honestly, though, what did Josh say about me?"

I pull a face. "Are you kidding? He won't even talk to me! He treats me like dirt."

Chloe wrinkles her nose. "Really? We'll have to change that. What did you do to make everyone hate you so much?"

"It's not what I did or didn't *do* . . . it's who I am. As a guy, I'm a loser."

Darcy puts an arm around me. "I'm sure that's not true."

"Trust me, it is. I don't fit in. Around here, that's the kiss of death."

Chloe squints at me and tilts her head. "Maybe we

119

haven't got the right look for you just yet. You need a stronger jawline."

"I'm afraid plastic surgery is out of my price range."

"I'm thinking a little shading through here." She leans closer and touches my jaw.

"Great! That's an excellent idea. I'm sure *makeup* will help with my credibility immensely."

Chloe leans back in surprise. "Why so snarky?"

"I'm sorry. It's just . . . kind of like information overload."

Darcy twists toward me. "Yeah? So what did you learn? Did you get any answers for your article? Dish!"

Sweet Darcy. She looks so eager. I want to give a full report, I really do, but somehow my brain won't cooperate. I want to talk about the rehearsal I just spied on—the stuff I saw and thought about—but all at once I have no idea how to formulate any of that into words. Here are my friends, turning to me with expectant faces, ready to listen, and I'm just sitting here with my mouth opening and closing like a goldfish.

Just then Darcy's ringtone goes off, distracting us from the report I can't seem to spit out. She reads the screen, a smile tugging at the corner of her mouth.

Chloe rolls her eyes. "It's Rob, isn't it? God, why doesn't he just leave you in peace?!"

Darcy flashes me an impish look. "He's been texting me all day."

"He senses she's moving on, so what's he do? Tries to lure her back. Dude's a little control freak."

I put my hand over Darcy's. "You're not going back with him, are you?"

She shakes her head, but I can see it's hard for her. "I'm resisting."

"Good. He's messed with you for too long—time to be strong."

"Yeah," Chloe says. "And he's not even cute!"

I look at my watch. "It's getting late. There might be a curfew in the dorms. I don't want to raise anyone's suspicions."

Darcy looks disappointed. "But you haven't dished yet."

"There's not much to tell yet." I feel suddenly exhausted, and the prospect of trying to recount the whole day is overwhelming.

"You okay?" Darcy studies my face carefully. She's always been attentive to my subtle shifts in mood; it's part of what makes her such a good friend. Right now, though, I just want to crawl under the covers and give in to sweet oblivion.

"Yeah. I'm just tired. It's been a long day."

"I guess this won't cheer you up." Darcy pulls a folder out of her bag and hands it to me. "But here's your homework from today."

"Thanks," I say, listless.

Chloe stands up. "Tomorrow I'll bring my makeup case. We'll see what we can do to make you more George Clooney."

Darcy jumps to her feet and holds out a hand to help me up. We go to the door, peek out to make sure nobody's there, then turn off the light in the prop closet and head out into the night. I walk them to their car, whisper a quick good-bye, and watch them drive away.

Now that the adrenaline rush of this weird adventure is wearing off, I'm starting to wonder if I can really hope to accomplish anything here. What if the entire mission is totally misguided? Maybe guys don't have any interesting secrets to reveal, even if they wanted to. Meanwhile, my real life will just keep piling up in my absence. I think of the homework assignments Darcy handed over. Maybe tomorrow during lectures I can get some of them done on the sly. There's no chance I can work tonight. Hopefully tomorrow everything will look clearer. Right now I feel so bone tired and my head's so full of half-formed ideas, I hardly know what I think about anything.

●●●●●●●●●●●●●●●●●●

Chapter Ten

●●●●●●●●●●●●●●●●●●

As I make my way up the empty stairwell toward my room, I start to feel butterflies swirling in my belly. I'm sharing a room with a guy I hardly know. Not just that: I'll be sleeping like five feet away from the sexiest guy I've ever met. I walk down the hall, listening to the night sounds: a TV explodes into laugh track, a bass beat pulses softly through the ceiling. In a matter of minutes I'll be in a very small space with Emilio. I'll have to figure out a subtle way to change from my uniform to the sweats and T-shirt I plan to sleep in. It's like going on a first date and knowing it's a sleepover.

There's no light visible under the door when I reach room 333. Using my key, I slip inside as quietly as I can, then lean against the wall a second, letting my eyes adjust. I pick up a scent in the air, a boyish smell of sweat and soap that I find oddly soothing. I stand there breathing it in, trying to get my bearings. After a moment I can make out the shape of Emilio under the covers. Our beds are lined up under the room's two windows. A faint wash of silvery moonlight has seeped in through the glass, and I can see the outline of his shoulder as he lies on his side.

I cross to the dresser I filled with underwear and T-shirts earlier that afternoon. Sneaking a glance back at Emilio's inert form, I hastily take off Tyler's blazer, tie, and button-down shirt. Hopefully he won't be in a hurry to get his uniform back; looks like I'll need it all week. Maybe I can get Darcy to bring me some white button-down shirts, at least. This one's not going to smell too pretty if I have to wear it every day. God knows how I'll manage my tie in the morning. Will Emilio think it's weird if I ask him?

Standing there in the dark wearing my undershirt and Tyler's pants, I hesitate. The original plan was to sleep in my two sports bra and tank top, but now I wonder if that's really necessary. The elastic in the double layers is cutting into my armpits. The thought of sleeping in even one is unbearable. Then again, what if Emilio wakes up and notices that his roommate has boobs? No matter how unspectacular said boobs might be, they'll still be very difficult to explain away. I'll just have to face the wall and keep myself covered up, then wake up before him and get dressed inside the shower stall where nobody can see.

Emilio makes a soft sound, a cross between a moan and a

124

sigh. I listen for his breathing. When I've convinced myself it's so steady that he has to be asleep, I hastily turn away and yank off my undershirt and both bras.

I'm naked from the waist up, digging around in the drawer for a baggy T-shirt when my elbow catches my toiletries kit on top of the dresser. It lands on the floor with a loud thud. Behind me I hear Emilio stir, and in an instant the bedside lamp floods the room with light. Panic surges through me as I instinctively cover my chest with both hands, cowering away from him.

"What the . . . ?"

"Scheisse!" My back still to him, I spot the T-shirt I need in the drawer. I yank it on, getting my head stuck in the armhole in my frantic scramble.

"What's going on?" He sounds drunk with sleep.

My head is still firmly lodged in the armhole, blinding me. I stumble away from the sound of his voice and stub my toe on the dresser, sending a searing arc of pain up my leg. "Ouch!"

"What are you doing?"

I somehow extricate my head from the wrong hole and force it through the right one. I still don't turn around, though, for fear he'll notice the boobage. "Everything's fine. Mind turning out the light?"

He grumbles something unintelligible but complies. Once the room returns to darkness I quickly shuck off my slacks and pull on a pair of sweats. My toe continues to throb. I limp over to the bed and dive under the covers, pulling them up to my chin and facing away from him.

Within minutes, Emilio starts to snore very softly. Careful not to make a sound, I turn over and study him, my body still carefully shrouded in covers. His face looks so innocent and young, one cheek smashed against his pillow. With each gentle breath his lips move ever so slightly, the tiny gap between them closing as he inhales, then opening again as he exhales, forming a miniature diamond of darkness between them. His dark eyebrows furrow briefly, then smooth out again.

Suddenly, as if responding to something in his dream, he casts off the covers so that most of his torso is exposed. No shirt. *Good God*. By now my eyes have fully adjusted, and the moon casts just enough light to see by. My eyes trace the lines of his shoulder, the place where his waist dips down and disappears into a tangle of sheets. I listen for his breathing, and when I've convinced myself it's so steady and even that he has to be sound asleep, I prop myself up on one elbow very carefully so I can get a better look.

Without warning, his eyelids fly open. I let out a little squeak of surprise before I can stop myself.

He sits up and glowers at me. "What?"

"What do you mean, what?" I clutch the sheets tightly to my chest.

126

"Why are you staring at me?"

"I'm not. I mean, I was, but just for a second."

He continues to pin me with his suspicious glare.

"I wanted to see if you were awake," I add lamely.

He snorts, fluffs his pillow, and collapses against it, facing the ceiling. "Well, I am now."

There's an awkward silence, during which I consider and discard a variety of possible comments to jump-start the conversation. This should be a dream come true: alone in the dark with an incredibly hot guy. Of course, I can't think of a single thing to say.

I'm beginning to wonder if he's drifted off to sleep again when he breaks the silence. "Where'd you go anyway?"

"What do you mean?"

"In the theater. I turned around and you were gone."

"Oh, that." My brain seizes up as I try to think of a plausible explanation. I go with the liar's rule of thumb: Stay close to the truth. "I didn't want to get in the way. Seemed like that girl was kind of, you know, into you."

He blows out a breath. "I don't know about that."

"She your girlfriend?"

I grit my teeth as I wait for his answer. Please, God, don't let him like Summer Sheers. I'll do anything, just grant me this one wish.

"No . . ." But his tone leaves a slight question still hanging in the air.

"What? You don't like her?"

"She's cool. And she's a good actress."

"You think?" It's out of my mouth before I can stop myself.

He sits up on one elbow. "Why, you know her?"

Scheisse! Backpedal, backpedal. "Oh, I just know *of* her."

"Really? How?"

I clear my throat, stalling for time. "Um, I have a cousin who goes to school with her."

"Yeah? What did your cousin say?"

God, how do I get myself into these situations? "She said Summer—that's her name, right?"

"Uh-huh . . ."

"I don't know, like she said Summer's from LA and did a lot of commercials, modeling, a few sitcoms, stuff like that, but that she's not really that good of an actress and if her dad wasn't in the business she never would have gotten all those parts."

Emilio considers this for a long moment. I said too much. Way too much. I need to have my mouth surgically removed.

"Sounds like your cousin's jealous."

It's my turn to sit up now. "No she's not!"

He holds up both hands as if to fend me off. "I'm just saying . . ."

"Summer's just not that good, is all." I lie back down. My

voice has been steadily getting higher and higher; I make a conscious effort to lower it. "According to my cousin."

"Girls say shit about each other," he says.

"So apparently you do. Like her, I mean." In spite of my best efforts, it comes out pouty.

He makes a strangled noise in his throat. "I don't know! Why are you so interested?"

"I'm not." Long pause. "I'm just making conversation."

Okay, enough about Summer already. She's stolen every role from me. Does she also have to steal the only guy I've had a crush on in ages?

Wait, what am I thinking? I can't crush on Emilio! He thinks I'm a dude. And anyway, this whole mission is about getting answers—real answers from real guys who think *I'm* a real guy. I can't let myself be distracted by some random attraction. Everything I saw tonight at rehearsal indicates that sexual chemistry is the main thing getting in the way of honest communication. I need to tame my libido and focus on my article. Since Tyler and company can't give me answers, and Josh's friends all think I'm too lowly to warrant a hello, Emilio might be my only shot at the truth. I need to work some of the seven questions into this conversation. How hard can that be?

Okay Natalie, concentrate. You need to be smoother than you were tonight at dinner. I deserve an Academy Award in the "awkward" category for that performance. How would a guy ask about this stuff? But see, that's the thing: He wouldn't. At least I don't think he would. I've got no idea what guys talk about when I'm not around because I'm— well, duh! Not around.

If I don't get a move on here he's going to fall asleep on me. I review all seven questions in my head and decide to start with number three. It's the easiest to bring up without sounding like a complete tool.

"Emilio?" I'm half hoping he'll be asleep so I won't have to risk making a fool of myself.

"Yeah?" his voice is husky.

I feel my pulse racing. "What do you, uh, look for in a girl?"

Pause. The same deadly pause I got at dinner. I can hear crickets chirping through the open window.

He fluffs his pillow and turns over onto his side, facing me. "What do I look for?"

"Yeah." Okay, so he's not immediately changing the subject to Blood Frontier, at least.

"You mean . . . in a girlfriend?"

"Right. What do you find . . . attractive?" I whisper this last word, marveling at the lines of his sculpted cheekbones in the moonlight.

"I don't know. I guess I like a girl who can be natural, you know? Be herself. It creeps me out when they try too hard."

I'm dying to point out that Summer is the *grande dame* of trying too hard, but I manage to restrain myself. Just listen, Natalie. He's telling you things. "Try too hard in what way?"

"Oh, you know. You can just sense it. Like when her laugh is fake and everything she says is all planned out. Like she's reading from a script. I don't like that."

"Yeah," I agree. "What else?"

He smiles, staring off into space. "Legs. I like long legs. Short girls don't do anything for me."

I want to jump up on top of my bed and do a victory dance; finally, being five eleven is coming in handy! Then I remember that Summer's almost as tall, and I deflate slightly. "Yeah. Legs are good."

"But the most important thing . . ." He pauses.

I can hardly breathe. "Yeah? The most important thing?"

"Is her ringtone."

"Get out!"

"No, seriously." He grins. "You can tell so much about a girl from her phone."

"You're so full of it."

"Not at all! Check it out. Girl's got a nostalgic ringtone, you know, like The Cure or some shit like that? She's trying way too hard to be ironic."

"Right . . ."

"If she's got the latest pop hit on there, also trying too hard, but in the other direction—like she thinks she's got to be super-trendy just to be liked."

"I can see that," I say grudgingly.

"Those ones that sound like alien spacecraft? Forget it. She might be fun for a little while, but pretty soon she'll be reading you your horoscope and spending every penny on 1-800-PSYCHICS."

"Sounds like you speak from experience."

He shudders. "And the reggae ringtone? Unless you want to spend every weekend at some dusty music festival where they sell patchouli soap and glass bongs, run the other way."

"Duly noted."

"It's all true." He nods. "The fine art of ringtone interpretation."

I smile up at the ceiling. The moon has cast an intricate pattern of shadows up there, and the wind stirring the trees outside makes the whole thing shiver. "Okay. So those are the red flag ringtones. Is there one you find acceptable?"

I sneak a sideways glance at him. God, he really is perfect. His skin is so gorgeous in the moonlight; like blue-tinged cinnamon.

"You know what I like?"

No, I think, *but please God tell me.*

"I like a phone that actually sounds like a phone. You know, that rings. Really rings. Like a phone."

I giggle, then hastily try turning it into a manly chortle. "Pretty old-fashioned of you."

"I guess so."

For a moment we both stare at the ceiling in silence, listening to the crickets, watching the shadows slide around the ceiling.

"Girls should just be who they are, you know? Is that too much to ask?"

I swallow hard. "Maybe."

He sighs. "Yeah, well, anyway. That's what I like, and I'm sticking to it."

"Thanks," I say.

"For what?"

"For being honest."

He rearranges his pillow roughly, flips over, and faces the wall. "If we're going to be roomies we might as well try to get along."

"Yeah," I whisper. "We might as well."

●●●●●●●●●●●●●●●●●●●●●

Chapter Eleven

●●●●●●●●●●●●●●●●●●●●●

𝒥n the morning, I wake up a little after six, creep silently to the bathroom, and take a shower in the far stall. Nobody else seems to be up yet, thank God. I towel off quickly and reluctantly pull on my double-ply too-small sports bras, the undershirt, and my tighty whiteys. Just add sock. Then I dress in the borrowed uniform and try for ten frustrating minutes to tie the tie. It's incredibly complicated. All I manage is a lame, lopsided knot that looks like a kindergartener's effort with a shoelace.

I come out of the stall, still rubbing my wet hair with a towel, wondering if I should use mousse in it or if that would seem too girly.

"You're a morning person too, huh?"

I scream. Okay, totally out of proportion to the situation, but I can't help it—I thought I was alone. Not only do I scream, I also jump like three feet into the air.

"Whoa." Tyler gives me an alarmed look. "What the hell was that?"

"Sorry. Little twitchy, I guess."

He stands at the mirror in sweats and a T-shirt, shaving. "Good thing I've got a steady hand or I'd have sliced myself to ribbons. Never heard a guy scream like that."

I bite my lip. It's too early to be a guy. I've never had a role I had to start playing the moment I rolled out of bed.

"Don't worry. I won't tell anyone." His eyes land on my tie and he cracks up. "What's that supposed to be?"

My fingers fly to the mangled knot and I can feel my cheeks burning.

"Here, I'll do it." He puts his razor down, wipes his hands on the towel draped over his shoulder, and reaches out to fix it.

I mumble my thanks while he loosens the knot.

"See, it's just over, under, up, around, up and through." He demonstrates. "You got that?"

"Uh . . . sure. Thanks for letting me borrow your uniform, by the way. You mind if I use it this week?"

"It's fine. This weekend I can show you where to buy one, if you want."

I nod, feeling a twinge of guilt, since by then I'll be long gone.

He must see something in my face, because he flashes me a knowing look and says, "Money a problem?"

"Oh, I—well, it's not that, I just—"

"It's okay. Not everyone here is rich, you know. I'm here on a scholarship."

I feel like a liar, but I take the path of least resistance. "Yeah, me too."

"Nothing to be ashamed of. All it means is we're here because of our brains, not our parents' bank account." He pats my shoulder. "See you at lunch?"

"Sure. Okay. And thanks again."

Later in the day, after I've made it through my morning classes without incident and eaten lunch with Tyler, Max, and Earl without making a total fool of myself, I'm starting to feel almost confident. It's one of those golden September afternoons, two parts summer, one part fall. The sky's a deep, flawless blue and the air smells of apples mixed with ocean. It's like the gods are saying yes to my crazy, harebrained scheme; they're saying yes to my pursuit of answers; maybe they're even saying yes to Emilio and me, though I've no idea how anything can happen with that, since—well, you know. Anyway, the point is I've almost survived my second day of school and a tentative trickle of optimism has started to bubble up inside me, the sense that I just might pull this off after all.

Then I look at my schedule. Suddenly the gods have stopped saying yes and have started making really obnoxious farting noises. In my face. With their armpits.

Fifth period PE.

I'm a pretty good dancer. I kick ass in yoga and Pilates. For some reason, though, in spite of the extreme hand-eye coordination that runs in my family, I'm a walking disaster when it comes to balls. I mean it: tennis, soccer, volleyball, baseball, football, cricket—any activity with a round or even semi-round object renders me a total klutz. We're talking dangerous levels of gawkiness. Seriously! I went to a party in the eighth grade at a bowling alley, and the birthday girl ended up with two broken toes because of me. Needless to say, we're no longer friends.

Something tells me PE at Underwood won't involve dancing, yoga, or Pilates.

When I get into the gymnasium the first thing I see is Josh and his minions shooting baskets. I actually feel like I might throw up. Because of my height, people have been trying to get me into basketball for years. That is, until they see me try to play. Once they stop laughing, they generally agree that b-ball's not my game.

To compound my anxiety, there's the issue of the locker room. My stomach churns when I realize I'll be expected to change in there. Luckily, the room is somewhat vast and cavernous, so I manage to find a dark corner where I can slip into the gym uniform I borrowed from Tyler without anyone noticing.

Coach Vroman is your textbook sadist. His beady eyes peer out from behind plastic glasses, obviously taking piggish delight in our pain. He leads us through a series of warm-up calisthenics, then unleashes a huge bag of basketballs on us and barks, "Layups!"

I look around, mystified, then line up behind my classmates. I don't know how to dribble the stupid ball, let alone force it into a graceful trajectory toward the hoop. Everyone else—even Max, with his matchstick legs and his scrawny arms—manages to charge forward, leap, and release the ball somewhere near the rim. I watch as Emilio slams it right down through the net with a satisfying swoosh. I feel like a lowly worm peering up at them as they hurdle their bodies through the air.

When it's my turn, I'm so panicked I can hear my blood pounding in my ears. I want to be anywhere but here—anywhere! What can I do, though? There's no escape. I bounce the ball a couple times and use all my concentration to keep bouncing it as I move forward. Okay, running's not an option, but I think I can walk and dribble at the same time. Bounce, catch, step; bounce, catch, step. Yes! I can do this.

I try not to notice that the entire gym has gone totally silent. Everyone's looking at me, but who cares? I'm doing this! I'm walking, bouncing, walking, bouncing. I'm almost under the basket now! All I have to do is shoot! In my excitement, I throw the ball down with more force than ever, feeling bad-ass. It ricochets off the floor at an angle and slams right into my crotch.

All around me, the room goes, "Ohhhh!"

I look up. Every face is staring at me, contorted into winces. Right. Ball in crotch equals excruciating pain. I'm such an idiot! Too late, I double over in pain.

"Ouch!" I yell. I sneak a glance around. Nobody looks convinced, so I add, "My balls!"

Okay, maybe too much? Another glance around tells me something about my performance is off. Josh has his hand over his mouth trying not to laugh, and Emilio is shaking his head. The coach blows his whistle and waves me over.

"Sorry, Coach," I say, jogging over to him. To my relief, the sound of squeaking tennis shoes and dribbling balls starts up again behind me. "My bad."

"New kid, right?" He studies me like I'm a fly in his soup.

"Yeah."

"Haven't played much basketball, I guess."

"Uh, not much, no."

"You hurt?"

If an injury gets me out of this, I'm in excruciating pain. My hand flies instantly to my sock. "Yeah. Pretty bad."

"You want to sit for a minute?"

"Okay."

"Over there." He nods at the bleachers.

I'm so relieved I could cry!

As I turn to walk away, he slaps me on the ass.

I spin around. "Hey!"

"Problem?" His sweaty face looks annoyed.

Just in time, I realize my mistake. The bizarre butt-pat ritual is totally normal among jocks. "No problem. Thanks, Coach."

On the way back to the locker room, Emilio jogs up beside me. "You okay?"

"I'm fine." I pick up my pace, head down, making a bee-line for my locker in outer Siberia.

I don't get very far, though. In fact, I've barely made it inside the door when a large pair of Nikes blocks my way. They're planted in a wide stance. The tan, muscular legs would inspire serious admiration under different circum-stances.

"What's up, spaz?"

I look up slowly. Josh stares down at me, face glazed with sweat.

I swallow, trying to remember how to speak. "Hey."

"Showers are this way." He jerks his head in the direc-tion of the group showers.

My eyes flick over to the showers involuntarily. A few of the guys are already in there, turning on the water, their naked butts shockingly white, and—*oh, God, I so didn't need to see that!* I feel a hot blush creeping up my neck.

"Good game out there." Josh leans in so close that I can feel little puffs of breath on my skin. "Man, your face is smooth as a girl's."

My hand shoots to my cheek. "No it's not!"

"How old are you? Twelve?"

As more guys file in, the smell of sweat fills my head, mixing with the steamy, soapy perfume of the showers. Voices bounce off the tiled walls and ricochet inside my head.

"Mayer, leave him alone," I hear someone say.

"Dude's like preadolescent." Josh goes on scrutinizing my face with a fascination that unnerves me.

Emilio comes over. "Give the guy a break."

I step back, adrenaline pounding through my veins.

"You defending your little girlfriend?" Josh taunts.

"Don't be an asshole," Emilio chides. "Guy's having a rough day."

Josh eyes Emilio another second, but backs off. I scurry over to my distant corner of the locker room and change out of my gym clothes as fast as I can.

That night in the prop closet I tell Chloe and Darcy about my aborted attempt to reinvent myself as Michael Jordan. They find it hilarious, which totally pisses me off.

"Oh, yeah," I cry, "laugh, why don't you?"

They do.

"Hey! I'm the one on the front lines here. I'm knocking myself out trying to get answers to *your* questions. I don't see you two doing much for womankind." I fold my arms over my chest and glare at them.

Darcy comes over and slings an arm over my shoulder. "Poor babe! We know you're suffering."

Chloe shrugs. "Doesn't sound so bad to me. A locker room full of naked Underwoodies?"

"Who were taunting me!" I remind her, indignant.

"Except Emilio." Darcy nudges me. "You like him, huh?"

"I—well—I think he's really nice," I say, flustered.

Chloe's jaw drops. "Oh my God! Natalie's got a crush! Natalie, you never like anyone."

I can't help grinning. "Okay, he's dreamy."

"And you're sharing a room with him!" Darcy pulls at her pink hair. "How hot is that?"

"It's very unnerving, actually!"

"Does he fart in his sleep?" Chloe wants to know. "I bet he does! Eugh! So gross. I take it back—you are suffering!"

"What is it with you and flatulence?" I say. "It's just gas—it's not deadly."

"Change of subject." Chloe clutches her stomach. "Unless you want me to puke all over the props."

"Yeah, actually, we need to focus." I walk over to a mirror propped up on one of the utility shelves and examine myself, finger-combing my hair. "How can I be more of a man? I need street cred."

Darcy comes over and examines my profile. "You could use some piercings."

"Not at Underwood. Try again."

"I've been doing a little research. I brought supplies." Chloe produces her aluminum makeup box from her enormous Louis Vuitton bag. She does makeup for the Mountain View High shows. She's really good at it. Now she undoes the latches, all business. "It should be easy. What you need is stubble."

"Stubble?" I can't help sounding less than enthusiastic.

"You're too baby-faced. They can't respect you if you look like a child. We'll just cut up some wool crepe"—she pulls a braid of brown, hair-like stuff from her box—"and apply it to your cheeks with stoppelpaste." She shows us a small tube of waxy-looking stuff. "I read about it on the Internet."

I consider this. "Will they be suspicious, though, since I didn't have any before?"

Chloe shakes her head. "Not at all. Guys grow facial hair. It's what they do."

"But can she sleep in it?" Darcy asks.

"Yeah, like do I keep it on all the time, or reapply it every morning?"

She pulls out a hair dryer and hands it to Darcy. "Warm up the stoppelpaste with this. Otherwise it won't go on smoothly." She's so focused on her task now, I wonder if she even heard the question. She's got scissors out and is cutting the wool into tiny bits.

"Chloe? This is kind of elaborate. I won't be able to do it on myself in the dorms. Can I sleep in it?"

"I'm pretty sure," she says. "If it gets funky I'll just touch it up each night after rehearsal."

I grin at her. "Thanks. You're the best."

She shoots me a look. "Whatever. You know I can't resist a makeover challenge."

It takes about forty minutes before Chloe will even let me peek in a mirror, but as soon as I do I can tell I look way better. The stubble adds a certain elusive, rugged charm to my face while simultaneously making my jawline stronger and more defined. I never realized how much a guy's overall attractiveness rests in his jaw. In a little over half an hour, Nat aged like three years and upped his hotness factor by several notches. He's no Zac Efron, but he's not bad.

"I should have thought of this earlier," Chloe chides herself as she adds another layer of tiny hairs, trying to perfect the look.

"It's okay," I say. "Nat's a work in progress."

We're all three scrunched together on the beanbag, since

there aren't any other comfortable places in the closet to sit. Chloe's using a big, soft makeup brush to apply the tiny bits of stubble to my chin. Darcy's curled up next to me, texting. It's nice being close to them, to tell you the truth. It seems like Nat never gets touched—well, unless you count Coach Vroman's pat on the ass today (cw!). Guys are way more careful about keeping their distance from each other, I guess. The Bay Area is known for its progressive sexual politics, but that doesn't necessarily change anything. It might be the most liberal place in the world; it's still weird for guys to reach out and make contact, which is kind of sad.

"I miss you two," I say softly.

"What are you talking about?" Chloe's eyebrows pull together as she applies another patch of stoppelpaste. "You've only been here two days and you've seen us every night."

"Time moves more slowly here. It reminds me of summer camp in that way—every day seems so intense."

Darcy looks up from her phone. "Because it's foreign. Your brain's trying to adjust. It was like that when I went to Israel with my mom."

"Yeah." I nod. "It's like I'm in a foreign country."

"Well," Chloe says, still concentrating on my stubble application. "While you were off in a foreign land, Darcy's been falling into bad habits again."

I turn to look at Darcy, but Chloe pulls my chin toward her again. "You're not back with Rob, are you?"

She cringes. "I had a brief relapse, but nothing fatal."

"They made out in the recording studio," Chloe reports.

"And I feel terrible about it, but we're not together or anything. He just—it was a moment of weakness." She stares at her lap. "I *miss* him. But I know I have to get over it."

I shake my head. Darcy deserves so much more than what he gives her. She knows it. I know it. We all know it. I guess sometimes it takes a while for the heart to get the memo from the brain.

I pat her knee. "You will. It takes time."

Chloe puts her makeup brush down and examines me, her eyes moving over my face like an artist skimming the canvas, searching for flaws. "I think you're done."

"Wait a sec," Darcy says. "I have something to contribute to Nat's new, manlier look too."

I put my hands over my head. "No more haircuts! It'll take forever to grow out as it is."

"Nope. Something much, much better." She smiles wickedly, reaches into her messenger bag, and pulls out an extra large pair of tube socks.

I laugh. "No!"

"Yes! Nat needs a bigger package."

"Oh my God," I groan. "I'm a junior in high school, not a porn star!"

Chloe nods solemnly. "She's right. You need a penile implant. Size does matter."

Let me just say it's late; we're punchy. We get the giggles. Chloe's holding me down and Darcy's on her knees, trying to zip up my fly after having just stuffed the enormous sock into my pants.

That's when we hear the closet door open.

We look up, startled. There's Josh Mayer, his expression utterly surprised.

For a second we all freeze: me with the absurd sock straining against my fly, Chloe using both hands to pin my shoulders against the beanbag, Darcy kneeling in front of me. We're quite the tableau, I'm sure.

Chloe breaks the silence with one of those suppressed laughs that sounds like a cat struggling to hock up a hairball. That sets Darcy off too. I cover my mouth with one hand, wanting to laugh but also terrified that we'll ruin everything.

Josh blinks once, says, "Uh, sorry to interrupt." Then he turns around, walks back out, and shuts the door behind him.

"Scheisse!" I whisper the second he's gone. "What do I do now?"

"Be cool," Chloe says. "I don't think he knows anything."

My eyes widen. "Really?"

She holds her hands up. "Who's to say Nat isn't hanging in the prop closet with his favorite drama sluts?"

147

Darcy cracks up again.

I look at my watch. "Oh God! It's ten fifty-six and curfew's at eleven. I've got to go!" I yank the sock from my pants and toss it at Darcy.

"Uh-oh," Darcy says, "there goes your manhood!"

"You guys are terrible!" But of course I can't really be mad. They're the best friends in the whole world. I turn to Chloe, a new thought just occurring to me. "You don't think this will screw up your chances with Josh, do you?"

She shakes her head, her expression blasé. "In my experience, a little competition never hurts."

I say my good-byes quickly and sprint all the way back to the dorms.

Chapter Twelve

*I*t's morning break and I drag myself over to the vending machine for really bad coffee. God, I miss Starbucks. I seriously think I'm going through caramel-soy latte withdrawals. I need caffeine though, even if it does taste like something excavated from a Dumpster and strained through an oily rag.

I tossed and turned for hours last night, my head filled with anxious dream fragments. They all featured Josh discovering me in various compromised positions and me getting kicked out of Underwood in disgrace. Emilio's face showed up repeatedly too, his eyes great dark pools of disappointment. Then I would wake and see him sleeping beside me, the beautiful lines of his body gilded with moonlight.

If there's a hell, I suspect it involves sleeping five feet away from somebody you're strongly attracted to but cannot touch.

Nobody's dragged me from my morning classes with accusations, though. That means either:

Josh suspects nothing.

Josh does suspect but isn't sure, so hasn't done anything about it.

Josh knows but hasn't ratted me out, at least not to administration. Yet.

Cradling my piss-poor coffee, I shuffle out into the courtyard, squinting into the dazzling sunshine. I spot Tyler, Max, and Earl seated at a picnic bench. They're still the closest thing I've got to friends, unless you count Emilio, and he's not anywhere in sight. I sit down next to Earl. He's poring over an astronomy textbook while Max and Tyler talk about *The Importance of Being Earnest,* which opens in two days. They have very minor parts; they play the servants of Josh's and Emilio's characters. Still, they're totally into it. I admire that. No matter how small the role might be, I still think you should play it with everything you've got. Even if you're the understudy.

Max's hair looks especially poufy this morning. It glistens like reddish gold cotton candy in the sun. "When Josh says, 'Merriman, order the dog cart at once,' he always forgets the second part of the line, 'Mr. Ernest has been suddenly called back to town.' If he does that Friday I won't wait for it—I'll just come in with my 'Yes, sir.' Otherwise it'll look like I screwed up."

"Try running sound," Earl complains, not looking up from his textbook. "Nobody ever gives me the right cue."

Tyler rolls his eyes. "That's because you're so picky. A cue is still a cue, even if it's not the exact words in the script."

Earl shakes his head in disgust. "That girl—the one playing Lady Bracknell?"

"Darcy?" Tyler says, then blushes. Just saying her name, he blushes! Interesting . . .

"She always gets that one line wrong. It drives me crazy."

Tyler frowns. "But she gets the gist of it."

Max gapes at him. "The gist of it? Is she trying to *improve* on Oscar Wilde's work? The poor man's spinning in his grave!"

"You sound like Mr. Pratt," Tyler says.

"Because Mr. Pratt is right!" And then Max blushes.

My, my. These guys may not talk too much about relationships, but they sure do blush at telling moments, don't they? Maybe that's the key to understanding the opposite sex; I could invent a science, call it blushology.

"Ow!" Max grabs his hand. "I just got a splinter from this stupid table."

"Oh, let me see." I reach across and cradle his hand in mine without thinking. "Hold on, I've got some tweezers."

"You have tweezers . . . on you?" Tyler asks, a note of disbelief in his voice.

"Sure." I dig through my backpack until I find the zippered hemp bag where I keep my essentials: ChapStick, Advil, Rescue Remedy, that kind of stuff. I locate the tweezers and pull them out. When I look up again all three of them are staring at me suspiciously.

"What?" I say.

"What is all that stuff?" Tyler asks, peeking into the pouch like it's full of tarantulas.

I feel a twinge of panic. I could have sworn I got all the tampons out of there. I look back inside the bag to be sure; yep, it's feminine hygiene product–free. Guys use tweezers, right? ChapStick is perfectly gender neutral. Why are they all looking at me like that?

"It's just . . . stuff," I say.

"Stuff?" Max echoes.

"Yeah." I deepen my voice and splay my knees wider. If it's possible to swagger while seated, I do. "Just shit I carry around. You got a problem with that?"

"Hey, Natman!"

I turn around and my panic gives way to incredulity. Josh and his entourage are strutting across the courtyard. They're all grinning at me like I just won *American Idol* or something. Wow. Who knew facial hair could be so crucial?

As Josh draws near he holds a fist up and I, unsure of what else to do, punch at it awkwardly.

"Dude!" he says.

I try a knowing laugh. "Dude!" I say back.

"Man, can I talk to you a minute?" His expression is conspiratorial.

I just chuckle. What the hell is going on? "Me?"

He punches my arm, laughing. It kind of hurts—actually, it really hurts—but something tells me not to bring that up right now.

"Sure." I get up from the table and follow him a little ways away from the others. I glance uncertainly over my shoulder at Tyler, Max, and Earl, but they look just as amazed as I feel.

"I don't know exactly what was going on in the prop room . . ." He trails off.

"With Darcy and Chloe?"

"Obviously, man. What, you think I wanted to quiz you about the inventory?"

I shake my head, trying to figure the best way to play this. "We were just messing around."

He nods, blue eyes boring into mine like he's trying to see into my soul. "Two at a time? I didn't think you had it in you."

I rub my jaw in what I hope is a man-of-the-world gesture, then notice tiny pieces of wool sticking to my fingers, which I hastily conceal in my pocket. "There's a lot you don't know about me."

He continues staring at me. "You're a freak."

"Hey—"

"But I like you. And so do the bitches at MVH, apparently."

I want to slap him for that, but stop myself. I'm finally getting somewhere with the upper crust; this is no time to ruin everything by giving in to feminist impulses. Instead I move my head back and forth like a cocky prizefighter. "What can I say? I got a way with the bitches."

I so can't believe I just said that.

He snickers. "Don't know what they see in you."

"I'm sensitive." I leer at him like this is code for something pornographic. "They like that."

He slaps me on the back so hard I nearly fall over. Then we walk over to join the others. Everyone looks at us with expectant faces, as if we're world leaders emerging from a summit meeting.

Josh nods at me, swipes me upside the head. "This guy's okay."

His friends laugh, but it's not the humiliating laughter I heard yesterday in the locker room. It's different. Their eyes shine with something like respect.

Here's the weird part: Even though I know it's all based on an absurd, convoluted misunderstanding, their laughter lifts me up like a warm, effervescent river and carries me right along. It's completely illogical and messed up, but after the beating my ego took the last couple days, it feels so good to do something right with these guys for a change.

Josh reaches out his fist again. I punch it with a little more confidence this time.

The chimes sound then, alerting us to the end of break. Josh leads his pack into the Hammond House, some of them turning now and then to get another look at me. I wink and flash the hang loose sign.

Tyler, Max, and Earl haven't moved. They're staring at me, slack-jawed.

"What?" I ask, all innocence.

"Nothing," Tyler says.

"I'll get that splinter out at lunch if you want," I tell Max.

"Sure," he says.

I go to grab my zippered pouch and the Rescue Remedy falls out.

"What's that?" Tyler asks, picking it up.

"Rescue Remedy. It's homeopathic. You want some?"

He thinks about it for a second, glances at the last of Josh's friends as they disappear into the building. "Sure."

"I'll take some," Max says.

Earl nods. "Yeah, me too."

In drama class, Mr. Pratt breaks us into pairs and asks us to perform scenes he's selected from various plays. To my horror and delight, he partners me with Emilio. I feel giddy when he hands us a photocopied scene between Antonio and Bassanio from *The Merchant of Venice*.

"I love this play!" I gush. "People don't do it that often because of the whole anti-Semitic thing, but it's got such cool roles."

Emilio looks a little surprised. "So you've read it, then?"

"Oh, yeah. I was in it."

He scans the script. "Who were you?"

"Portia," I blurt without thinking.

His dark eyes fasten on my face. "Isn't that a girl?"

I have to think fast. Something about Emilio makes me let down my guard, which is something I can't afford to do here. "Yeah, she's a girl. I mean, she plays a guy for one scene, but . . ." I get distracted by the weird wobbly feeling his intense gaze produces in the pit of my stomach. Concentrate, Natalie! "We did it the way they did in Shakespeare's day—you know, with guys playing all the roles, even the female ones."

"Really?" He studies me with even more interest. "Wasn't that kind of embarrassing? Playing a girl, I mean?"

"No way," I say, indignant. "A great role is a great role."

Emilio appears to consider this. I wonder what he's thinking. Have I lost all manly credibility with him now? Did I ever have any to begin with? God, why did I bring it up? Step one in making your roommate think you're a complete freak: Admit you not only played a girl but enjoyed it. Great, now he'll probably get all homophobic on me and sharing a room will be totally awkward.

"That takes *huevos,* man," he says at last.

"Sorry?"

"Huevos, cojones." When I still look at him blankly he clarifies. "Balls. Nobody gave you shit for that?"

I feel myself swelling with pride. He thinks I have *cojones!* Okay, it's a twisted sort of compliment, given my actual anatomy, but the point is he respects me. "Sure, some people did, but I didn't worry about it."

Mr. Pratt comes over to check on us. "Have you read the scene?"

I shrug. "I know the play pretty well."

"Yeah, me too."

I look at Emilio in surprise. He elbows me. "What? I can read! I like Shakespeare."

"Okay, great." Mr. Pratt rubs his hands together, dark eyes shining. "So Antonio and Bassanio. What do you know about these two?"

"They're friends?" I offer.

"That's right," Mr. Pratt says. "In fact, these guys have a friendship most of us only dream about."

Emilio nods. "Antonio's totally got Bassanio's back."

"Right! How do you know that exactly?" Mr. Pratt asks.

"Because he risks everything for Bassanio," Emilio says. "He's already invested all his money in those ships, so he's

157

got nothing, but when Bassanio shows up he's like, 'Sure, use my credit.'"

Mr. Pratt looks pleased. "Exactly! That's how much Antonio loves his friend, right? He's willing to risk his life just to be sure Bassanio can have whatever he needs." He pauses, taking us both in. "Do you have any friends like that?"

We're both a little taken aback by the question. It's a classic drama teacher move, though; one minute you're talking about Elizabethan merchants, something totally removed from everyday life, the next you're being asked to reveal your innermost secrets. That's how they get you to play a role convincingly—by connecting the experiences of the characters to your own.

I glance at Emilio, who just studies his hands, brow furrowed.

"Friends like what?" I know what he means, but I'm stalling, unsure of how to answer. Natalie has friends she'd do almost anything for, but Nat? Nat has Tyler and company, who are better than nothing, but I hardly think I'd give up a pound of flesh for them.

"Friends you'd risk everything for—even your life."

Emilio still doesn't look up, but he says, "I guess I used to, back home. Not really here."

"Yeah," I say, relieved to have an easy way out. "Me too."

Mr. Pratt looks from Emilio to me and back again; I can't

read the expression on his face, exactly. It's some complicated combination of concern and compassion, I think,
Who knows, though? Maybe he's just thinking about his
next cigarette.

"So imagine, then, or remember the friends you had before. Concentrate on that feeling—respecting and caring
about someone so much, you'll do anything to make them
happy. Yeah? You got that?"

We both nod as some roughhousing across the room
draws Mr. Pratt's attention. "Hey! Careful, duckies. You
knock over that suit of armor and you're dead." He darts
across the room, fingers raking through his unkempt hair.

In spite of the swelling noise all around us as guys rehearse their scenes, an awkward silence settles between us.
I make an effort to break it. "You want to be Antonio? You
seem more like him."

He grins crookedly. "How so?"

"I don't know." What I mean is that Emilio has Antonio's style. He has a certain poise and dignity you just
don't see very often, especially in males under thirty. He
has Antonio's gravitas, his regal bearing. I don't say any of
this, of course. Instead I mumble, "You just seem more
mature."

"Okay, cool. So you're Bassanio—the dude who's so
whipped he'll risk his best friend's life just to get a good
look at Portia," he teases. "Cold!"

"No, man. It's not like that." I try on a little swagger. "I'm just confident with the ladies, is all. I know she'll fall for me, so it's not really a risk at all."

"Whatever you say." He treats me to one more lopsided grin before we pick up our scripts and start to rehearse.

Chapter Thirteen

That afternoon I sit on my bed, hunched over my notebook and scribbling furiously. The side of my hand is ink-stained, but I'm concentrating so hard I barely even notice. My head is filled with a jumble of messy thoughts, half of which are splayed haphazardly across the pages. I'm trying to get it all down, no matter how crazy or illegible the sentences might be. I write about watching Chloe and Darcy at rehearsal the other night—how different they seemed from the girls I know and love. I write about the weirdly exhilarating power I felt today when Josh and his friends looked at me with such respect, even though that respect was totally misguided. Mostly, though, I write about Emilio: his smell, his eyes, his laugh. In some ways I feel so at ease around him, so free and weirdly myself. That doesn't make any sense, though. He doesn't even know my real name.

I've been here three days, and still I don't have any of my seven burning questions answered. At this rate, it's hard to imagine I'll have enough material to fill out one good paragraph, let alone a lengthy investigative article. I mean, yes, I have plenty of thoughts, observations, and Emilio-fantasies to jot down in my journal, but none of that qualifies as investigative reporting, does it? And yeah, I could write a *ha-ha, look at the clever prank I pulled off* type piece, but that's not really journalism, is it?

The phone on the nightstand rings, making me jump. Emilio's at the library. It has to be for him—nobody I know has this number. I stare at it a moment. What if it's Summer? Would she recognize my voice? I tell myself not to touch it, then watch as my hand snakes out and snatches it up on the fourth ring.

"Hello?" I'm careful to pitch my voice in the guy register.

On the other end, a long stream of Spanish erupts. The voice is female. It doesn't take a linguist to figure out she's crying and swearing. My stomach drops. Does Emilio have a girlfriend he never mentioned—maybe someone back home? I sit up straighter and grip the phone with both hands.

"Uh, I'm sorry, but this isn't Emilio," I say when she takes a breath.

Pause.

"Who is this?" Her English has a faint accent; she sounds suspicious.

"Nat Rodgers. I'm his—"

"*Ay Dios,* you're the new roommate, aren't you? *Mierda!* I'm so sorry. I hope you don't speak Spanish."

"I don't," I reassure her.

"I'm Erica, his sister. I got so used to him being alone, I forgot all about you." She laughs, but I can still hear the tears in her voice. "How embarrassing! Is he there?"

"No. He's at the library." Now that I know she's his sister and not his girlfriend, I find I like her much better.

"Oh. That's why his cell's off, I guess." Her disappointment is palpable.

"Is it an emergency? Do you want me to run over there? I could have him call you in a few minutes."

She sighs. "Oh, not really. Just, you know, relationship drama."

"I hear you." It seems presumptuous to offer my services as emergency hotline counselor, and yet I'm reluctant to just hang up. She seems so upset. "Guy trouble, then?"

"Yeah." With that, she bursts into tears. It sounds like the kind of crying that's been going on for hours; she's a little hysterical, the poor thing.

When she seems more in control I say in a tentative voice, "Do you want to talk about it?"

She goes silent for a beat. I guess my offer must surprise her. "What's your name again?"

"Nat Rodgers."

"I feel bad. You probably have homework and—"

"No, really." I look at my notebook, filled with pages and pages of barely legible notes. It's not like I'm going to spin that straw into literary gold any time today. "I'm not that busy."

"It's my stupid boyfriend, Julio. He's such a *capullo,* he broke up with me and I'm the last to know!"

An hour later, I have the full story. Apparently, Emilio's from East LA. It surprises me that he never mentioned that, though I'm not sure why; I should know by now that guys don't always volunteer even basic information about themselves. Erica took the GED last spring and became an au pair in Sausalito. Her boyfriend, Julio, was still in LA, but had promised to move north as soon as he'd saved enough money. They planned to rent their own place in the city, since Erica was having a tough time with the family she worked for. She liked the kids but hated the mom. Anyway, the despicable Julio started seeing Erica's best friend—or ex-best friend, as of today. Erica heard it from her cousin, who spotted them kissing at a movie theater last night. Every now and then Erica lapses into a quick burst of mournful Spanish, which makes it more tragic, somehow.

It occurs to me that in one conversation with Erica I

learned way more about Emilio's family than I've gleaned after living with him for three days.

"You're such a good listener." She's just recovered from another good cry, during which I made soothing sounds the best I could. "Better than Emilio, even! He would've lost patience by now."

"Oh, no," I say, "it's nothing."

"You got a girlfriend?"

"No." Oh, God. All at once this entire conversation seems like a very bad idea. "I mean, yes. Sort of. It's complicated."

"You must be very popular with the girls."

"No, I'm a disaster with girls."

She chuckles. It's a low, husky sound that reminds me a little of Emilio's laugh, except femmier. "Come on! You know how many guys can deal with a girl in crisis? Almost none. And you *offered*! Most boys would run screaming, they hear somebody's sister crying hysterically on the phone. I really appreciate it."

"No problem," I mumble. My cheeks are burning up. She's totally *flirting* with me.

Emilio walks in then, looking incredible in faded jeans and a black T-shirt. The sight of him fills me with lust and relief in equal parts. I jump up and shove the phone at him. "It's your sister."

"Erica?" His brow furrows.

"Yeah." I don't want to be rude, though, so I say into the receiver hastily, "Hey, here's Emilio, see you later!" before pressing the phone into his hands again.

He looks puzzled. I'm too embarrassed and panicked to explain, though. Besides, I figure he'll appreciate a little privacy. I wave good-bye and duck outside, then clamber down the stairs. I do a couple laps around campus, breathing in the warm, salty air and glancing up occasionally at the puffy clouds drifting overhead like brilliant white ships.

I let myself back into our room about twenty minutes later. For some reason, nervousness thrashes around inside my belly like a trapped animal. Emilio is at his desk studying his lines. He looks up at me and smiles.

"So, you met my sister."

"Sort of," I mumble.

"She was impressed."

I try making a dismissive noise in my throat. I hope it's man-speak for *I don't want to talk about it.* No such luck. Emilio either doesn't understand the cue or willfully ignores it.

"You know, Josh is having a party Friday after we open."

I don't say anything. Under different circumstances, hearing a guy I like broach the subject of a pending party would get me all fluttery for sure. Somehow, though, I doubt Emilio plans on taking me as his date.

"I wasn't really invited," I say.

"So, I'm inviting you."

"Isn't it for the cast?" I don't know how big Josh's house is or how many guests will be there, but if Summer is one of them, I can't risk going.

"The cast, and the people they invite." He picks up a Nerf football and starts tossing it back and forth. "Maybe you'd like to take my sister."

I just raise an eyebrow.

He laughs. "What's wrong? Just one girl too boring?"

"What's that supposed to mean?"

"I heard about the prop closet."

I groan. "Wait, you heard about that and now you're fixing me up with your sister?"

His face goes serious. "She's not that kind of girl."

"So then why are you—?"

He waves a hand at me dismissively. "Just because you like to have fun doesn't mean you can't treat a nice girl the way she should be treated. Am I right?"

"Yes. True. But the whole prop closet story was—"

"None of my business. Which is why I didn't bring it up."

I think about that. "Wait, but you did bring it up."

"Whatever. You're getting hung up on details. The point is, I scored you a date with my sister. That's no small thing. She's beautiful. And she's the sweetest. You're going to thank me."

"I'm sure she's great, but . . ." *But I'm a girl. A straight girl. And the only person I want to go out with is you.*

"What?" His expression darkens, and a muscle pulses in his jaw. "You don't like Mexican girls?"

"Oh my God, no!" I cry. "Nothing like that. I'm just . . . shy."

He pauses, considering me. To my relief the anger drains from his face, replaced by an earnest, confiding expression. "I'm her brother, which means I don't let her go out with just anyone. Take it as a compliment. Anyway, it's not like you have to marry her. Just distract her—she's really upset over this Julio guy. *Hijo de puta.* I'm so going to kick his ass."

"I'm honored," I say, truthfully, "but this Friday isn't going to work."

"Okay." He nods, unfazed.

"Great. Thanks for understanding."

"How about tomorrow night?"

"Emilio!"

"What? You can take her out to coffee. It's a three-dollar, two-hour commitment, tops."

I sigh. It's starting to look like there's no graceful way out of this. I'm already so tangled up in lies, what's one more tiny deception?

"All right, tomorrow night."

"That's my man." He puts out a fist and I punch it.

He goes back to studying, and I hunch over my note-book once again. My thoughts are more jumbled than ever, though. I can't eke out even one decent sentence.

"Are you taking Summer to the party?" I blurt before I can stop myself.

He looks over his shoulder at me, surprised. "Maybe. It's not really that kind of deal."

"What kind of deal?"

"The whole cast will be there. It's not like I have to invite her." He squints at his script again.

"You do like her though, right?" I run a hand through my hair, thinking of how much longer and sexier hers is.

"I don't know. I heard she has a boyfriend."

"Robbie Herbert," I say quickly, not thinking.

He turns around to face me. "How do you know?"

"Um, well, I heard that, anyway."

"From who?"

"Uh . . . where did I hear that?" Think, Natalie, think! "My cousin! Remember, she goes to school with her."

"Oh yeah. You said that." He stares moodily at the floor.

I fiddle with my pen. "Are you in with love her?"

"In *love*?" He says it like it's a completely foreign con-cept. "I don't know, man."

When I dare to look at him, he's eyeing me suspiciously. I guess the L-word isn't used much among people with Y chromosomes.

I try to remedy the slip with a dash of manliness. "Would you tap that ass?"

He's just taken a sip of water and he almost chokes. "Oh, man, don't."

"What?"

"Look, I know English is your first language and everything, but don't go messing with booty slang until you've got the hang of it, okay?" He shakes his head, grinning. "'Would you tap that ass.' That's just *wrong*."

I find myself smiling back, glad to be done with the subject of Summer Sheers. "Okay. If you say so."

"And go easy with my sister. You don't need to be tapping nothing until you know her better—maybe not even then."

I roll my eyes. "Believe me, you've got nothing to worry about."

If only he knew.

Chapter Fourteen

"*P*sst! Nat. You awake?"

I'm dreaming, of course, fast asleep. Rachel Webb and Chas Marshal ask me in snide tones where my Story of the Year entry is. I slap it onto the table before them in triumph, thinking, Ha! That'll show 'em. Their eyebrows arch in unison. I look down to see what I've presented is a bulky pair of tube socks.

"Nat? Wake up."

My eyes fly open. There's a figure towering over my bed, fully dressed. I flinch, startled.

"It's okay. It's me, Emilio."

"Wha? Arrgh." I'm always very articulate at—I blink at the clock—two in the morning.

"Come on." He crouches beside my bed. I notice, even in my groggy state, that he's so close I can smell the salt on his skin. That wakes me right up.

"Where are we going?" I ask.

"It's a surprise."

Okay, I know this is dangerous. Surprises aren't exactly welcome when you've got everything to hide. The excitement in his voice is contagious, though. I find myself rolling out of bed. As usual I've gone to sleep in sweats and a hoodie, for maximum boob camouflage. All I have to do is pull on my tennis shoes.

"Seriously? You won't tell me where we're going?" I whisper.

"Just follow me."

We say nothing and try to move without sound as we make our way down the stairs and out the back door of the dorms. Once outside, the warm night air envelops us, smelling of pine and dry grass. Even now, in the middle of the night, the heat of the day clings to the parched earth. Every few minutes, though, a breeze wafts inland, carrying with it the cool, moist kiss of the ocean.

"This way," Emilio whispers.

I follow him down the footpath that leads to the New Media building, but before we've gone far he veers toward the forest.

"Where are you taking me?" I ask again.

"I told you. It's a surprise."

We walk a little farther without speaking, just the sound of the crickets in our ears and the occasional hoot of an owl. Our feet move soundlessly through the spongy, well-manicured lawn.

When we reach the edge of the forest I hesitate. "Are we going in there?"

I can just make out his white smile in the darkness. "You scared?"

"No."

"Well, then, shut up and follow me."

I can't see that I have much choice, when he puts it that way. The last thing I want is for Emilio to think me a wuss. I crave his respect more than anyone I've ever met in my life.

Whoa.

I flash on all my crushes before this, from the unnamable longing I felt for Todd Wright in the fifth grade to the halfhearted interest I took in Paul Pacaud last summer. I wanted them to like me, to lust after me, to worship me, even, but for some reason respect wasn't a huge consideration. I was too busy trying to seem hot to ever be myself. Now, stripped of my lip gloss, my shiny hair, all my girly trappings, the thing I want most from Emilio is for him to get who I am and respect that.

There isn't much time to analyze this train of thought further, though. It takes all my concentration just to follow his faded yellow T-shirt through the maze of shadows and trees. The moonlight can't penetrate the thick canopy of foliage, and I can barely see. As we walk, every snapping twig, every flurry of movement in the underbrush has me jerking my head around, jumpy as a cat. Once, a bat swoops close to my face and I can't stifle my yelp of surprise, though it sounds babyish, even to me.

"Easy there, cowboy." Emilio chuckles softly.

"A bat almost got caught in my hair!" I say indignantly.

"So naturally you scream like a girl."

We go on walking, and eventually we're able to move side by side instead of single file. The trees are less dense, and a little moonlight trickles through the branches, casting patterns of silver lace here and there on the ground. Our footsteps fall into a rhythm, the cadence so exact we could be one person. Neither of us says anything for a while. This is how guys do it, I think: less conversation, more action.

In the distance, I can just make out the gentle gurgle of running water. I cock my head.

"You hear that?" he asks, sounding happy.

"Yeah. What is it?"

"We call it Dead Man's Creek. Don't know if that's the official name or not."

I shiver. "Why do you call it that?"

"Don't know. To scare the freshmen, I guess. Or maybe because of the corpses they're always finding there."

"The—?"

He laughs and starts running ahead. "Come on! We're almost there!"

It's hard keeping up in the dark. Emilio's fast, his agile form weaving through the trees and bounding over rocks like a fleet-footed stag. Luckily, I'm a much better sprinter than I am a basketball player, so I run as fast as I can and manage not to lose him.

I'm not sure how deep into the forest we go. All I know is just as I'm starting to pant and wheeze, wondering how much longer I can keep it up, we pass under a big redwood tree and stop short.

"What do you think?" Emilio asks, sounding maddeningly unaffected by our race. "You like it?"

There before us is a swimming hole, about twenty feet in diameter. Its banks are studded with rocks and ferns. The glossy surface glitters in the moonlight. It's breathtaking.

"Yeah," I murmur, strangely touched. He wanted to show me this—me, and nobody else. "It's—wow."

"I know! Isn't it awesome?" He starts peeling off his shirt, his movements hurried. When he reaches to unbutton his jeans I grab his arm.

"Wait! What are you doing?"

He looks puzzled. "Going for a swim."

"Now?" My voice sounds strangled. "Here?"

"Yeah, of course. Why, what's wrong?"

My mind races. "Um, is that a good idea?"

"It's still warm out. Why not?"

I rack my brain for a way out of this. "It is. Warm. It's just that . . . well, in my family, um . . . this will sound stupid."

"Don't worry—just say it."

Even as I open my mouth, I'm not sure what will come out. "We're religious."

"Uh-huh . . ."

"Very old-fashioned. Practically Amish."

He looks confused. "Okay . . ."

"And very modest. I mean, like no nudity. Ever. In our house."

He widens his eyes in sudden understanding. "Is that why you took a locker way the hell away from everyone else?"

"Uh-huh."

"And why you never change when I'm in the room?"

I nod. This is so good! I've unwittingly stumbled on the perfect explanation for my chronic fear of nudity. "You noticed? Yeah, that's why."

His brow furrows. "So you're like . . . ashamed?"

"Well, you know how it is when you grow up a certain way, and . . ." I trail off. Since there have never been any guys in our house, my mom and I have always been very clothing-optional. In the summer, we're practically nudists. I decide the less I say about this fictional puritan

176

family of mine, the better. "It's just awkward for me."

"Okay." He stands there, bare chest gleaming in the moonlight, one button of his fly undone. I feel a distinct swoon coming on, but I keep it under control.

"You think I'm a freak?" I ask quietly.

"No, man, not at all." He claps me on the back. "Listen, we just won't look, okay? Once we're in the water you can't see anything, anyway."

My heart pounds. "You promise not to peek?"

"What do you *think*?" He shoots me a look, adding, "Like you've got anything I'm interested in."

It's risky. The water looks so smooth, though, so inviting. I've worked up a sweat during our run, and I can just imagine how great it'll feel, slipping into those cool depths. Besides, to refuse him now would be all wrong. Bringing me here was his gift to me; not getting in would be like throwing that generosity back in his face. I'd rather blow my cover and forget about Story of the Year than do that.

"Okay," I say, "but you go first."

"I'm on it." He unbuttons his fly and drops his jeans.

Through sheer willpower I manage to close my eyes.

Okay, I peek. But just once.

Then I hear him splashing around and laughing, so I know it's my turn.

"Don't look!" I order, trying to sound threatening.

177

"I told you." His voice ripples across the water. "You're not my type."

I huddle in the shadow of the big redwood tree and tear off my clothes with superhuman speed. I don't bother to fold anything, just fling my clothes onto a sprawling fern and dash for the swimming hole, using my hands to cover as much of me as I can.

"*Scheisse!* Ahhh!" I let out a little scream when I hit the water. God, what's up with that? I never realized I made so many involuntary girly sounds. I seriously need to get a grip! It's colder than I'd expected, though. I feel that initial pang of shock, the breathless *why the hell am I doing this?* Then my body shivers once and surrenders to it, letting it surround me and make me weightless. Delicious.

"Nat?" I hear him about ten feet away, but can barely make out the shadow of his head bobbing in the water. "You okay?"

"Yeah." I laugh—okay, giggle, then try to disguise it as a grunt. "It feels great!"

"Told you." He swims toward me. I can see the concentric circles radiating from him. *Oh, God, why do you torture me?* The urge to swim right up to him and feel the cool velvet of his skin underwater is overwhelming.

He stops about five feet away. The water's deep; we tread it for a moment in silence. I want to float on my back and relax, but I'm afraid too much of me will show. It occurs to me that this is exactly the sort of quiet, unguarded moment when I should be working through my list of questions to see if I can get some honest answers. I'm starting to think the list of questions isn't exactly the best approach, though. Too awkward and formal. Maybe just being here, experiencing what guys experience, is enough.

"It's colder than I expected," I say, shivering again.

"Yeah? Is that what the squeal was about?" I can tell he's trying not to laugh. "Listen, man, don't take this the wrong way, but you scream like that in East LA, you're sure to get your ass kicked."

I splash him in response.

After a pause, he says, "I never really fit in there."

"Where?"

"In El Sereno, where I grew up." His voice is different, now—more serious.

"Why not?" I ask.

"Just didn't, you know? My best friend back home, Gustavo? He's a dealer now. Not the hard stuff, just pot and X, but still. It pisses me off, man. I so can't relate. It's like I can't even go home and feel at home, you know? I'm stuck between worlds."

"Yeah. I can see that." A part of me thrills at the chance to be his confidante; something tells me he doesn't talk like this very often. Another part of me writhes with guilt. The guy he's confiding in doesn't even exist.

"You're the first person I really wanted to talk to here," he says.

My throat feels tight. "Yeah?"

"Yeah. I hate giving up my privacy, but if I have to have a roomie, I'm glad it's you."

"Same here."

We tread in silence again, listening to the symphony of crickets punctuated by the occasional croak of a somber bullfrog. I wonder what he would say if he knew my secret. Would he like Natalie as much as he likes Nat? Would he tell her his secrets?

Yes, I tell myself. *Nat is just Natalie in pants. The person he likes is* you.

Deep down, though, I'm not so sure.

Chapter Fifteen

Thursday morning I wake to the sound of Darcy's personalized ringtone—"Super Freak," at her insistence. The frantic, tinny rhythm slowly infiltrates my brain, a crew of disco inferno elves hacking at my skull with tiny pickaxes.

I force my eyes open with great effort. The first thing I see is Emilio sprawled beautifully across the crisp white sheets, his broad brown back half illuminated by the spill of amber light slipping through the curtains. Again with extreme effort, I tear my gaze away from that delicious sight and manage to locate my cell on the nightstand.

Rolling over to face the wall, I whisper into the phone, "This better be good."

"Where were you last night?" Darcy cries about four decibels louder than I can bear. "Why didn't you meet us after rehearsal?"

Still half asleep, I tumble out of bed, shuffle across the

floor, and shut myself into the small closet Emilio and I share. "I didn't know where to meet you. The prop closet hardly seems safe now."

I can hear her saying something to someone else, then, "Chloe says you're paranoid. Did Josh say anything about the other night?"

"Yeah."

"Oh my God! What did he say?"

I rub my forehead. "I got like four hours of sleep last night. Think you might stop screaming at me?"

She takes no notice. "Tell us!"

"Okay, okay!" God, girls are so demanding. "Josh and his friends think I'm a total player now."

"Seriously?" She reports to Chloe, then returns to me, laughing and breathless. "That's too precious! How's the facial hair working out?"

I touch my cheek. Hmm, not so sure the swim last night did my stubble any favors. "Actually, ask Chloe how to touch it up if—"

Suddenly the door swings open and light pours in. I squint up at Emilio, who stares down at me with a bemused little grin.

Quickly, I cough and force my voice into a more masculine register. "I'll figure something out."

Darcy pauses a second, then bursts into maniacal laughter. "You're getting pretty good at that."

"Yeah, I can't talk now. See you later." I end the call and stand up, hunching over so my boobs won't show in my oversized T-shirt. It got too hot for the hoodie last night. "Morning."

"What the hell are you doing in the closet?"

I shrug. "Didn't want to wake you."

He's wearing just his boxers again. I can make out the subtle etchings of a pillow pattern on the side of his face. Somehow it makes him even sexier. As I walk past him my arm accidentally brushes his; electricity sparks across my skin. I pretend not to notice and keep walking, even though I desperately want to look for signs in his face that he felt it too.

"I'm awake." I think I can detect the slightest huskiness to his voice.

Does he sense it—this crackling energy between us? If so, what does he make of it? If he's attracted to me as Nat, does that make him gay? God, the whole thing is so confusing. My groggy, pre-coffee brain struggles to keep up.

"Everything cool?" he asks.

"Yeah."

"You reporting back to the mother ship?"

"Just some girl I know."

He raises his eyebrows. "Should I tell Erica you're taken?"

"She's a friend."

183

"Uh-huh. So you're not planning to 'tap that ass,' as you put it?"

I shrug. "Not in the immediate future, anyway."

He chuckles, then stops abruptly. He peers at my face, leaning toward me slightly. I'm overcome by self-consciousness about my morning breath. My God, is he going to kiss me? Is this seriously happening? His hand moves in slow motion toward my cheek. His fingers extend, floating closer, a look of concentration in his eyes. I lick my lips, hoping they're moist and kissable; my eyes flutter closed. I pucker up, heart pounding . . .

"Dude, what's up with your face?"

My eyes fly open. "What?"

"Your skin—it looks, like, waxy or something."

My face burns, probably turning the attractive hue of a rotten tomato. Both of my hands fly to my cheeks, covering as much as I can. Without answering his question, I dash to the mirror hanging on the back of the closet door. *Scheisse!* The water from last night's swim has rendered my five o'clock shadow a mess of waxy, flaking bits. The tiny hairs are bunched up in random spots like a cheap sweater that's started to pill.

Panicked, I race down the hall to the bathroom. Disgusting odors fill the air; several guys are busy relieving themselves at the urinals. These details barely register, though, as I run to a sink, turn on the water full force and scrub at my face. Since I was in too big a hurry to grab a washcloth, I have to use the rough brown paper towels from the dispenser to get the remaining stopplepaste off.

"Hey, Rodgers. Whattup?"

I turn and see Josh is one of the guys using a urinal. He jerks his head in greeting. I force my eyes away from what's in his hand, flash an awkward smile, and go back to my scrubbing. Please, God, don't let him notice the tiny clumps of hairy wax I'm frantically washing away.

"How's the mack daddy today?"

"Fine," I say, distracted.

I've almost got my face clean now. It's distinctly less manly than it was yesterday, but at least I don't look like a walking lint brush. A drawn-out farting noise comes from one of the stalls, followed by several plops. I cringe in disgust.

"Listen, want to hang at lunch? I got a couple things I want to ask you."

Good Lord, Josh is still peeing! He must have a bladder the size of a beach ball. The guy could irrigate a small country! I can't help staring, fascinated by the golden stream that continues to flow unabated.

"You okay?"

"Huh?" I shake my head, force myself to focus on his face. "Sorry, still waking up. What did you say?"

Finally, mercifully, he gives the trouser snake a little shake and tucks it into his boxers. "You free at lunch?"

"Uh, sure."

"Cool."

I examine my pink, freshly scrubbed face one last time in the mirror and hightail it for the door.

I sure hope this morning isn't an omen of the day ahead. Nobody should be exposed to so many horrors before eight a.m.

At lunch, it's a little awkward telling Tyler, Max, and Earl that I won't be sitting with them today. Their faces cloud up when I stop by their table and, casually as I can, mention I've been summoned by Josh.

"It's no big deal," I add with forced insouciance. "He just wants to ask me something."

Tyler shrugs, matching my tone. "Whatever."

Max mumbles something under his breath.

"What?" I ask him, leaning a little closer.

"I see how it is. Too good for us now." He stares at his turkey sandwich, refusing to meet my eye.

I'm a little surprised to realize just how eager I am to prove him wrong. When I first got here, I considered these guys social barnacles I had to pry off if I wanted to get in with the crowd that mattered. Now, strangely enough, I find myself actually caring about what they think; in fact, their opinion matters more to me than Josh's. I wonder when *that* happened.

Natalie wouldn't even think twice about a handful of pimply misfits. She'd follow her hormones straight to the hotties. Nat's a different story. Still, the fact remains that I'm here to get answers, and my little geek-boy trio here can't provide me with much when the only girl they know anything about is Lara Croft.

"I'll be right back." I try without success to get them to look at me. They all feign fascination with their food.

Frustrated, I take my tray to Josh's table, where the buzz and banter instantly hushes and I'm greeted by silent, knowing nods. They're still looking at me like I'm some sort of god. It's amazing what a little *ménage à trois* action in the prop closet will do for a guy's credibility. Needless to say, it wouldn't have the same effect on a girl's rep.

I walk over to Josh, trying not to blush when I consider what they're all picturing. The guy next to Josh scoots over instantly, making room. I set my tray down and have a seat while Josh slaps me on the back.

"Natman, what's happening?"

"Nothing much. You wanted to see me?"

He nods, chewing his sandwich and regarding me thoughtfully. The way his jaw works in slow, determined circles reminds me of a cow. I thought he was so cute when I first saw him at the mall; now that I know him better he's a lot less attractive. It's weird how seeing someone like Josh through a guy's eyes changes everything. I'm not so blinded by his perfect skin or his athletic build. Now he just looks like a self-satisfied prick with a mammoth ego.

"What do you think of Underwood? You like it here?"

I nod, wondering where he's going with this. "It's great."

"You moved here from out of town, right?"

I nod again, taking a bite of my coleslaw. The guys around us have resumed their conversations, but they shoot us covert glances now and then.

"So, uh, how do you know Darcy and Chloe, if you don't mind me asking?" He frowns, waiting for my answer.

"I . . . met them through my . . . cousin."

"Your cousin?"

"Yeah." Man, this cousin of mine sure does get around. "She's friends with them."

Josh leans back in his chair, folds his hands behind his head. "Look, I'm not sure how to ask this, so I'm just going to say it straight out. Are you like *with* Chloe, or was that just a one-time thing?" When I don't answer right away he jumps in to elaborate. "Not that it's any of my business. It's just, you know, I think she's kind of hot, and I've been working on her for a while now, so I'm just wondering—"

"Working on her?" I stare at him.

"You know . . ." He looks slightly uncomfortable. "Getting to know her. Greasing the wheels, so to speak."

I'm not sure what sort of look I give him, but it must convey disapproval because he jumps in again, eager to clarify. "I haven't touched her, dude, I swear. If she's yours, tell me and I'll back off. But I figure not many guys get it on with their actual girlfriend and her best friend, so maybe you're not, you know, into her . . . like that."

"You want permission to move in on Chloe?"

His smile tells me I'm testing his patience. "Permission? Not exactly. I just want to know the score."

My mind is a mosh pit of clashing impulses. Chloe likes Josh, so I should give him the answer he wants. If I imply I've got some sort of claim on her, that would be working against her best interests.

On the other hand, just sitting next to this guy makes me feel slimed. His flashing blue eyes, perfect complexion, and silky smooth voice all make me inexplicably queasy.

Still, it's not me who has to like him. It's Chloe. Is it my place to interfere when she's into him?

Then again, she doesn't know him like I do. All she sees is Mr. Suave, the same guy I'd see if I was a girl. Naturally, I *am* a girl, but—anyway. Shouldn't I use my inside knowledge to help my friend? Isn't that part of why I'm here in the first place—to enlighten girlkind?

This is getting incredibly confusing.

"So you really like her?" I study him carefully.

"She's hot."

"But do you *like* her?"

He jerks his head back, his face creasing with alarm. "I don't know."

"Look, I'm only asking because she's kind of a friend and I don't want to see her get hurt."

He rips off two-thirds of his sandwich with his teeth and says between chews, "A friend? I guess! The scene in that closet sure looked friendly enough."

"You still haven't answered my question."

He glances around, bored. "I'm not looking for a girlfriend. She just seems like a good time."

"Uh-huh."

He raises an eyebrow. "You can still do whatever you want with her—I just want to borrow her for a night or two."

That's it. Internal debate officially over. This guy's going down.

"I get it. Well, in that case, let me give you some pointers."

He grins. "Right on. I knew you'd be cool."

"There's something you should know about Chloe." I lower my voice to a conspiratorial whisper and he leans in. "She's got this weird fascination . . ."

"Awesome . . ."

"With flatulence."

"Farting?"

"Uh-huh. Totally turns her on."

He raises an eyebrow. "You expect me to believe she likes gas?"

"She does! I don't know what the story is, but my cousin told me she's into it, so I gave it a shot. We were just hanging out and I let one rip."

He laughs. "No way."

"Yep. She's been into me ever since."

He makes a face. "That's kind of gross."

I shrug. "Chick's weird. It's like she got this idea somewhere along the way: Real men have gas, and they're not afraid to let it out."

"You swear you're not messing with my head?" He studies me, his face suddenly grave.

I cross my fingers behind my back. "Swear."

He holds my gaze a moment, as if deciding whether or not to believe me.

"How do you think I got in with her? Without insider information, a guy like me could never touch that."

He hesitates another half second, then nods. "Thanks, man."

"No worries."

"I owe you one."

I stand with my tray and head back toward my usual table. "This one's on the house."

Chapter Sixteen

I've agreed to meet Erica at Java the Hut around nine tonight, after she puts her little monsters to bed. I can't believe I'm actually going on a date with Emilio's sister. It's so deeply, intrinsically wrong I want to scream. Still, it can't be helped. I tell myself it could shed more light on my research, though how going out with a girl will reveal the inner workings of guys, I'm not exactly sure. I'm grasping at straws—I see that. The real reason I'm going out with Erica is because of my pathological need to please Emilio. He could ask me to set my hair on fire and—let's face it— I'd at least consider it.

Since the play opens tomorrow night, the cast has dress rehearsal jitters. Their call is at six. It's five thirty now, and I've managed to secure my spot on the catwalk, hidden from view. Emilio told me he and Summer are meeting early tonight to run lines. Naturally, I couldn't resist the temptation to torture myself by spying on them.

So far, though, my spying hasn't revealed much at all. They really are running lines—speeding through them in the flat, emotionless tone actors use when they're just reassuring themselves they know every word. Of course, it's a great relief to see there isn't some steamy behind-the-scenes romance going on. Not at the moment, at least. I find myself getting kind of sleepy and bored, just sitting up there while they recite their scenes in monotone murmurs. Last night's swimming hole adventure left me simultaneously exhausted and wired all day.

That's when Summer interrupts the speed-through with something that wakes me right up.

"This is where we kiss," she says casually.

Emilio looks at her uncertainly. "Right . . ."

Just so you know, it's totally not the norm to run blocking when you're doing a speed-through. There's no time. The whole point is to rattle off the lines as fast as you can without pausing for anything. That's why it's called a speed-through—hello!

"I think we should run that," she clarifies. "I'm not sure we've got it right."

"Uh. Uh, okay." Emilio looks distinctly uncomfortable. "The lines, or . . . ?"

"No, the kiss." She unfolds herself from the chaise longue with maddening dancer's grace and crosses to where he's been pacing nervously stage left. One finger trails down the front of his shirt while she gazes up at him, all innocence. "We want it to be perfect, don't we?"

I could kill Summer Sheers! I could just throttle her skinny neck with my bare hands. Riveted by the sight of them, faces drawing nearer, I mutter under my breath, "Beeatch!"

"Now, now, let's not be catty."

I practically jump out of my skin! Jerking around, I see Mr. Pratt standing calmly beside me. Where the hell did he come from? A quick glance back at the stage tells me neither Emilio nor Summer noticed. They're locked in a kiss that could steam your pores wide open.

Gleghh! Did not need to see that.

"Mr. Pratt," I say, forcing my eyes away from the train wreck below. "I didn't hear you come up."

"Nat, I'm going to ask you a question. I want to make it clear you can be honest with me, okay?" There's a gentle quality to his voice I never noticed before. Spying on his rehearsals or sitting in his Dramatic Literature class, what struck me most was his sardonic, bossy manner. Now, though, his soft brown eyes search my face with an imploring look.

"Sure. Go ahead," I whisper, desperately cutting my eyes to the stage to make sure Summer and Emilio can't hear us.

Mr. Pratt notices this and lowers his voice even more, speaking into my ear. "Why are you up here?"

"Uh, because . . ." Improvise, Natalie, improvise! "I really want to be an actor but I'm too shy." I say this in such a rush the syllables tumble over each other and practically render the sentence unintelligible.

He nods, his face unreadable. For a long moment his eyes lock on mine, and I fear he's pulling some sort of Jedi mind trick. It's like he can see right into my soul. Finally, he breathes, "That's bullshit."

"Wh-what?" I stammer.

"We both know why you're up here."

"We do?"

He just nods solemnly, his eyes urging me to fess up. God, what's he saying? Does he know I'm really a girl? Does he have some sort of hypersensitive director's intuition about these things? How long has he known? Will he blow my cover? My mind backflips through these frenetic questions like a coked-up cheerleader.

"Nat, everyone has feelings they're uncomfortable discussing."

"Right . . ." Where's he going with this?

"Some of us can pick up on those feelings, though. We understand them. You see what I'm saying?"

"Maybe." I dart a glance back at the stage. Still kissing. Shoot me now.

"I just want you to know that whatever's going on inside your head, it's probably normal."

I nod uncertainly.

He lowers his chin and gives me another meaningful look. "I'm going out on a limb here, because I was once in your shoes. A nice old guy did the same for me, so I'm returning the favor. Let's be honest; you're here because you have feelings for Emilio."

Blood rushes to my face. "I—well—we're roommates."

He closes his eyes a moment, as if in sympathy. "That must be very challenging."

"No, he's great. I mean . . . we're friends."

"Nat, you do realize it's a dead end, right?" He puts his hand on my back in a fatherly way.

"What is?"

"You can be friends all you want, but at the end of the day you've got to face that a guy like him"—he nods at Emilio—"is never going to be interested."

I steal another look at the stage: still kissing! Very open-mouthed kissing. Man, is she trying to swallow him whole?

"I can see it's difficult for you," Mr. Pratt whispers, "but you've got to face facts. Emilio Cruz is as hetero as they come."

I just nod, unable to speak.

"Someone like Max, on the other hand . . ." He trails off, but his expression says it all.

"I see what you mean," I mumble. My mind is racing. It's much better he think I'm gay than female, sure, but he's so kind and sincere I feel like a total schmuck deceiving him.

"Not that you have to act on anything until you're good and ready," he adds urgently. "Believe me, you've got your whole life ahead of you."

"True."

"Once you're out of high school, the world opens up like a, like a . . ." He searches the air, then gestures before us like he's conjuring a magical tableau. ". . . a curtain rising on the first glorious scene."

"Wow. Cool."

He nods again at Emilio and Summer on the stage. Their lips are finally starting to separate, their bodies peeling apart reluctantly. I feel like I've been punched.

"If you keep falling for the Emilios in this world, you're going to make it hard on yourself. That's all I'm trying to say."

I swallow, forcing the words out. "Yeah. I see what you mean."

"Do you?" He slaps my knee. "Excellent! So glad we got to chat."

"Thanks."

Not only am I crushed after witnessing the sickeningly gratuitous, steamy rehearsal kiss, now I also feel guilty about lying to Mr. Pratt. He so clearly just wants to help; that's something too few adults can honestly claim. How do I repay him? By totally deceiving him. I'm a first-rate *scheisse*.

Not long after he's left me alone to lick my wounds, something happens to distract me from my misery. Chloe stumbles into the theater, clutching her stomach and looking ill. She's followed immediately by Josh.

"Chloe! What's the matter?" Josh calls after her.

Chloe makes an incredulous sound. "You're disgusting!"

"Come on, don't be like that."

Mr. Pratt, who has just climbed down from the catwalk ladder, puts on his reading glasses to study a clipboard. "What's the problem, duckies?"

"She's fine," Josh says, wrapping an arm around Chloe, who pushes him away. "There's no problem."

"He farted!" Chloe says, pointing at Josh accusingly. "Super-loud!"

Mr. Pratt sighs and scribbles something on his clipboard. "Let's try to act our age, people."

"You don't understand," Chloe says, one hand over her nose. "I have a weak stomach."

Just then Josh farts. Chloe yelps and runs out the side doors. The rest of the cast, most of whom have straggled in by now, titter.

"Mr. Mayer, are you having gastrointestinal difficulties?"

Josh nods. "Kind of. I ate seven bean burritos."

Oh my God! I bite my fist to keep from cracking up. I don't know whether to feel guilty or exultant. I settle for a little of both.

"Good Lord." Mr. Pratt runs one hand over his face. "All right, enough with the sixth-grade antics. Come on, people. Chop-chop! We have a show to put on!"

During the dress rehearsal, Chloe, Darcy, and I communicate via text. They're not in very many scenes together, so when one is busy the other is usually available, creating a sort of tag team text session that's imperfect but nonetheless serviceable. We agree to meet up in a little alcove behind the theater during their ten-minute break at intermission. Of course, it would be more convenient to meet in the bathroom that's been designated the girls' dressing room, but we can't do that because Summer could barge in at any moment, struck with the sudden urge to admire her luscious hair.

How I hate Summer Sheers right now! She doesn't know the real Emilio. She's just kissing him because he's cute. I'm willing to bet she doesn't have any idea that his sister is heartbroken, or that his childhood friend Gustavo is dealing drugs, or that he has a theory about ringtone interpretation. She doesn't deserve to kiss him! Her aim is to turn him into another accessory. It's all about her. Summer's way too self-absorbed to comprehend the deep, rich magic of Emilio Cruz. She has no idea what it's like to lie beside him in the moonlight staring at the shadows on the ceiling, or how his voice sounds as it spills across the surface of a deep, still swimming hole at three a.m.

As we crouch in the shadowy alcove littered with illicit cigarette butts, I can smell Chloe's breath; she reeks of Altoids. I'm guessing she chomped her way through several dozen to combat the sour aftertaste of vomit. I feel a slight pang of guilt, knowing I'm at least indirectly responsible for making her puke. She and Darcy are both in costume. They wear elaborate dresses with high, lacy collars, dainty gloves, and massive hats. Darcy's hot pink hair is covered with a gray curly wig; Chloe's hair drapes over her shoulders in elaborate sausage curls.

Chloe hands me a pink striped Victoria's Secret shopping bag. I refrain from commenting about her choice of containers—surely, though, she could have chosen something less conspicuous, given my circumstances.

"What's this?" I ask, peeking inside.

"Stoppelpaste, wool crepe, scissors, makeup brush—everything you need for your five o'clock shadow."

"So you can look hot on your date," Darcy adds, nudging me. I texted them about meeting Erica later tonight, which they find hysterical. So glad my misery amuses them.

"You don't think people will notice I keep sprouting and losing my facial hair randomly?"

Chloe sighs and another whiff of curiously strong minty-ness hits me. "I told you, that's what boys *do*—they get hairy, they get unhairy, repeat."

"And eat bean burritos until they burst, apparently." Darcy giggles, turning to me. "Did you hear about Josh?"

"I witnessed some of it from the catwalk." I hope I don't sound as culpable as I feel.

Chloe covers her mouth, as if the very mention of it makes her want to puke all over again.

"What was he *thinking*?" Darcy wonders aloud.

"What did he say about it?" I ask.

Chloe narrows her eyes to slits; for a moment I think she knows it was me, but then I realize her hostility is aimed at Josh. "He claims he did it for me! He heard I have a thing for guys with gas. Can you imagine? Talk about misguided!"

"Listen, Chloe, I've been meaning to say something about Josh . . ."

She blinks at me. "Yeah?"

"Well, I kind of know him a little better now. As a guy?"

"Uh-huh . . . ?" Something about the way she says this warns me she's less than receptive.

"He just wants to sleep with you!" I blurt in a rush.

"Wait, what are you talking about?"

"Don't fall for him, okay? He doesn't care about you as a person."

A light dawns slowly in her caramel eyes. "Wait a second. *You* put him up to that, didn't you?"

"Not exactly . . ."

"You did too! You deliberately fed him misinformation. Why would you do that?"

"Chloe, I know it seems weird, but—"

"*Weird*?" she echoes, pissed now. "It doesn't seem *weird*. It seems psychotic!"

"I was trying to help!"

Darcy places one hand on Chloe's shoulder and the other on mine. "Everybody calm down."

"He thinks you're a slut!" Okay, not my most tactful moment, but Chloe's rising anger makes me nervous. "That came out wrong. Sorry. I had to do *something*."

She shakes her head at me in disbelief. "You're jealous."

"Whatever."

"Why else would you be such a bitch? Just because a cute guy likes me and not you doesn't mean you can get in the way!"

Darcy looks from Chloe to me with increasing helplessness. "You guys, please don't fight."

"Yeah, Chloe, that's it." My tone is now edged with bitter sarcasm. "I'm *jealous*. Sure wish I could have guys like Josh lining up to *use* me."

"Shut up!"

"I have inside information," I say, frustrated. "Trust me, he's sketchy."

"Trust you?" she scoffs. "Yeah right, after the stunt you pulled? Ha!"

A door at the back of the theater swings open, and I shrink farther into the shadows instinctively. Mr. Pratt peers across the darkness in our direction.

"Girls? Why are you *skulking*? You better not be smoking—it's hell on your voice, not to mention your complexion. Intermission's over. And I don't want you out here in your costumes anyway. Chop-chop!" He disappears and the heavy door slams behind him.

"Come on, Darcy." Chloe gives me a dirty look before flouncing off.

"I'll work on her," Darcy mutters, squeezing my hand. "Got to go. Good luck tonight!"

"Thanks."

I trudge back to the dorms, ineffectually attempting to keep the bright pink Victoria's Secret bag hidden under my blazer. I get several weird looks from the guys I pass, but try to ignore them. I feel totally confused and defeated. Guess that's the last time I'll try protecting Chloe from an opportunistic scumbag. Fat lot of good it does me. God, what a fabulous evening this is turning out to be: gender identity counseling from Mr. Pratt, the repulsive stage kiss by Summer and Emilio, hated on by my best friend. And now, as my reward for enduring all this, I get to go on a date with my soul mate's sister.

Did I say soul mate? I meant roommate.

Obviously. If Emilio were my soul mate, he would never kiss Summer like he did tonight.

Would he?

●●●●●●●●●●●●●●●●●●●●●●●●●

Chapter Seventeen

●●●●●●●●●●●●●●●●●●●●●●●●●

$\mathcal{I}$ barricade myself in the dorm room, knowing Emilio
will be at rehearsal all evening, but locking the door just
in case anyone else happens by. It takes me almost an
hour to get the stubble thing right, and even then I'm
not one hundred percent sure it looks authentic. The
whole time, my mind keeps playing snippets of the day
in quick flashes like a bunch of random film clips spliced
together: Chloe's eyes narrowed to slits, Josh farting,
Summer standing on tippy toes for her kiss, Mr. Pratt
blinking at me in sympathy. All of us have our wires
crossed and crisscrossed so many times it's impossible to
untangle the mess. It really does seem like the entire human race might as well be conversing with hand gestures
and grunts, for all the success we're having. I thought the
main chasm was between men and women—guys and
girls, whatever. Now that Chloe's so pissed at me just for

trying to protect her, I'm starting to wonder. Maybe all human beings are destined to misunderstand each other, regardless of our chromosomes.

It's so hard to be truly honest with people, and even when you are there's no guarantee they'll appreciate it. I think about my Dr. Aphrodite column. For more than a year I wrote what girls wanted to hear—what *I'd* want to hear in their shoes. It was so easy, I didn't even know I was doing it. People would much rather be fed candied lies than bitter truths. Who knows? Maybe that's the natural order of things. Chloe sure as hell would be happier right now if I'd just let her go on thinking Josh really cared about her. Who am I to go against nature, insist the mating dance change? Maybe illusion and artifice—lies, even—are a necessary part of romance.

As I'm brushing on another layer of stubble, my eyes fall on a photo Emilio keeps taped to the corner of the mirror. He looks about thirteen; he's at the beach, his arm draped casually over the shoulder of a chubby-cheeked kid about his age. They both wear sunglasses and matching Batman T-shirts. This must be Gustavo, his best friend from home. I think of our night at the swimming hole, when he told me about Gustavo and how hard it's been for him to make friends here at Underwood. Once again, that mixture of uneasiness and longing swells up inside me. I know there's something real between us—a fragile bond we can barely afford to acknowledge. Yet that bond is built on a foundation of half-truths and lies.

That's the thing I can't quite figure out. I'm obviously not being honest with him; he doesn't even know my real name! Yet somehow, in spite of that, I feel more myself around him than I've ever felt around any guy.

How does that even make sense? I'm totally lying to him, and that enables me to tell the truth? It's a conundrum wrapped in an enigma.

I'm still fretting over these questions like a dog chasing its tail when I finish my facial hair application and check myself one last time in the mirror. I've traded my Underwood uniform for street clothes: a black T-shirt, button-down shirt over that, and the boy jeans I got at Macy's with Darcy and Chloe. I pose for myself a few times. Once I've assured myself no boobage shows, I try to decide if I qualify as hot. Even with the facial hair I'm still a long way from rugged, but some girls might consider me attractive in a slightly effeminate, nerdy sort of way. I add a blue baseball cap at the last minute, hoping it might render me a little more butch.

I drive off campus into town and park in a dark corner of the lot behind Java the Hut, thinking what a disaster it would be if someone (my mom, for instance) recognized my car and decided to pop inside for a chat. I picked this place in particular because nobody I know ever goes here; it's a little grungy and the baked goods are inevitably stale. It's a few minutes after nine as I come in through the back door, quickly scanning for familiar faces.

To my relief, there's only a twenty-something barista behind the counter with a book, a middle-aged guy glued to his laptop, and a girl about my age sitting alone in the window, sipping a 7UP nervously.

As I approach, trying hard to walk like a guy, she stands, smoothing her hair.

"Hi, I'm Erica." She wears an electric blue blouse, jeans, and rhinestone jewelry. She's short—maybe a little over five feet tall—and curvy. Her long dark hair has been carefully arranged with pretty rhinestone clips. She has Emilio's eyes, except hers are about three shades lighter, milk chocolate to his semisweet.

I offer her my hand. "Nat Rodgers. Nice to meet you."

"Thanks for not hanging up on me the other night."

"Oh, no problem."

"Most guys would have run screaming." She smiles a pretty smile and sits back down. "Glad I didn't scare you away."

I try to ignore the guilt I feel about fooling her like this. She radiates hope, expectations, a palpable optimism that makes her seem needy and delicate as a baby bird. Here she is, looking at me with eyes wide, mascara-darkened lashes blinking. I feel sick.

"I'm going to get some coffee." I gesture vaguely at the counter. "You want anything?"

"No, I bought myself a soda." She looks down at her lap. "I didn't know if you'd show."

Is it my imagination, or was that a subtle reprimand? God, did I screw up already? I'm like seven minutes late and I lost points?

"I can pay for it if you want," I say, awkwardly pulling some dollars from my pocket.

Her disdainful look tells me my potential boyfriend score dropped again. Pretty soon I'll be below zero. "That's okay. Really."

I hurry away from her, shooting a wistful glance at the exit. God, I so don't want to be here. Obviously I don't want her to *like* me like me—that would make things even more complicated than they already are. All the same, it's a bit humiliating to be judged ineligible within five minutes of meeting her.

I order at the counter, pay the bored barista, and fill my coffee cup with decaf. In the meantime, I sneak a couple glances at Erica. She spots her reflection in the plate glass window and furtively tries to rearrange one of her clips. I feel a pang of empathy, knowing that self-conscious anxiety that permeates first dates. I want to tell her to relax, she looks fine, but I know it won't help. Why do we girls obsess over our appearance so much? It's like we really believe getting our hair and makeup just right will make all the difference. As if any guy worth our time would fail to see our beauty because a rhinestone clip is arranged at a wonky angle.

I come back to the table with my coffee, this time determined to make a better impression. She's bound to give Emilio a full report, right? I don't want her telling him I'm a complete loser.

"So," I say, taking a seat across from her, leaning on one elbow in what I hope is a suave yet sensitive posture. "How are you feeling about the thing with Julio?"

Bingo! This appears to be my one selling point as a date: a willingness to listen. I figure it worked for me on the phone, I might as well try it again. Sure enough, like a racehorse hearing the shot, she's off and running, telling me all about the warning signs she ignored, the series of small betrayals leading up to this huge one, the debilitating fury she feels whenever she thinks of him. All I have to do is nod and murmur.

I can see the resemblance between her and Emilio. Her face is fuller, her features softer, but there's a quality to her smile—a certain radiant warmth—that reminds me of him completely. She sure is a lot more forthcoming than he is, though. Her willingness to dish is one hundred percent female. As she moves from Julio to her life story in general, I perk up, anxious to learn more about Emilio's past. In half an hour I gather way more information about the Cruz family than I learned from Emilio all week. She tells me about the other brothers and sisters (all five of them), their father's death six years ago, their mother's obsession with Emilio becoming a doctor. It's like Emilio showed me a bare-bones sketch, while Erica offers up a full-color portrait. And yet I can't say Erica's version is more intimate. Emilio doesn't say much, yet there's a depth and a power to the things he does share. Every time he's revealed something to me over the past week, I've had the profound sense of having earned something precious.

Eventually, Erica pauses in her monologue and blushes prettily. "But I've been going on and on about myself. What about you?"

"What about me?"

My temporary reprieve from the scoring session is now over. Her brown eyes bore into me once again, searching my boyfriend potential with the intensity of lasers. "What do you like to do?"

"Uh . . ." My mind goes utterly blank under her scrutiny. "I don't know."

She purses her lips. Definitely not the right answer. "Do you play sports?"

I scoff. "Me? Yeah, right! No, I'm super-clumsy."

"Do you party?"

"Not much," I say. "Beer makes me stupid."

"So what do you do?" She folds her arms across her chest, daring me to impress her.

"Well, let's see . . ." I feel so paralyzed by her expectations. It's terrifying. I decide to stick close to the truth. "I like to act—do theater—mostly drama, though occasionally musicals." That doesn't sound manly enough, does it? I backpedal. "But only the edgy musicals, not the sappy ones. Musicals with lots of death and destruction in them—hard-hitting social themes."

Her expression doesn't change. I plow on.

"Oh, and I like to write. I think I want to be a journalist. Professionally, I mean. Though who knows? It doesn't pay very well. And I might not be good enough."

"What kind of stuff do you write?"

"Mostly about relationships," I say automatically.

"Relationships?" The slant of her eyebrows tells me this is suspect.

I can understand her skepticism; I liked this guy freshman year until he told me about his passion for self-help books. Hearing him talk about his inner child was such a turn-off.

"Between governments," I amend, "political parties—not like *love* or anything. Is that what you thought I meant? No, I leave that stuff to you girls."

At this her eyebrows shoot straight up. "What 'stuff' exactly?"

"You know, hearts, flowers, romance. Us guys don't get into that shit."

All at once she looks crushed. Two seconds ago she was the stony-faced director at the audition where you act your ass off and don't even earn a curt nod; now she's the baby bird again, tears pooling at the base of her lashes, threatening to ruin her carefully applied mascara.

Instinctively, I lean forward. "What's wrong?"

"You seemed different on the phone."

"Different, how?"

Her bottom lip quivers. "Sensitive."

It's at this moment that I recognize afresh the insanity of my situation. Here I am, working extraordinarily hard to impress this girl, someone I never wanted to go out with in the first place. Yet every moment I sit with her I get drawn further into her web of expectations. She has this enormous power—the ability to pronounce me man or worm—yet the guidelines about how to win her favor are maddeningly unclear. She wants me tough as Vin Diesel yet cuddly as a kitten. How can I be both at the same time? How did I even get roped into trying?

These thoughts evaporate when I glance up and see who just walked in. Emilio. And two steps behind him, in her signature boots, blond hair shining like a shampoo commercial, smile bright as a Whitestrips ad, is Summer Sheers.

!!

Instantly I drop to the floor.

"Nat?" I hear Erica say. "What the . . . ?"

Okay, this is bad. I'm crawling around amidst straw wrappers and scone crumbs. There's no way I can get to the door without Summer recognizing me. I'm screwed.

"Um, seriously," Erica says, peering under the table at me. "What are you doing down there?"

Step one: Stand up. *Thwack!* My head slams into the underside of the table. Jesus Christ! Since when do I specialize in slapstick? I force myself to ignore the throbbing pain and stagger to my feet.

"Contact lens," I mutter. "Popped right out."

"Did you find it?"

I don't answer; I'm too busy clocking Emilio and Summer's progress in my peripheral vision as they head toward us. One false move and Summer will know it's me. I keep my back to them. Erica looks from her brother to me in startled confusion.

"I've got to go," I mumble.

Erica frowns. "Go? Where?"

"Hey you two," Emilio says from behind me, but I refuse to turn around.

"I'll call you," I mumble to Erica. No idea where that came from—just seems like the thing to say. Then I dart for the door, my head low, grateful for the baseball cap.

"Where you going?" Emilio asks. "Hey, Nat!"

I pause at the door, still not daring to turn around. "Sorry—an emergency," I say in the deepest, least recognizable voice I can manage, before scurrying outside, heart pounding.

Chapter Eighteen

*E*milio gets back to the dorm minutes before curfew. I've had almost an hour to cook up an excuse for bolting; I've even rehearsed it in front of the mirror a couple times, trying to strike just the right balance between explaining and groveling.

I'm sitting on the bed with my cell at the ready; as soon as I hear his footsteps in the hall I snatch it up. He lets himself in and I glance up, trying to look distracted, as if I'm thoroughly embroiled in a heated discussion that's been going on way too long.

"No, Mom . . . I'm sorry, but I don't think I can make it to the funeral. . . . It's such short notice, that's why. . . . Well, I think Aunt Marsha will understand, don't you? It's almost midterms. I can't just fly to Chicago tomorrow! I've got class."

I risk a peek at Emilio. He's taking off his shoes. I can't read his expression.

"Okay. I love you too, Mom. Bye." I put the phone down and force the air from my lungs, hoping to sound depleted and mildly depressed. "Sorry I had to bail on you guys so abruptly. My uncle died. Mom called to tell me while I was hanging with Erica."

Emilio looks up. "Really?"

"Yeah. Terrible. He's been sick for a while, but nobody thought he'd go this soon."

He appears to mull this over as he peels off his shirt. God, does he have to do that right this second? I need all my concentration to keep my lies straight. He's merciless, though. Completely oblivious to my squelched whimpers, he unbuttons his jeans and lets them drop to the floor. Burgundy boxers hang loose on his hips. His body couldn't be more divine.

"That's weird," he says.

"Mm?" I tear my eyes away from his rippling abs.

"Erica said nobody called while you were at the café."

"Called? Did I say called? I meant texted."

"She said you never even looked at your phone." It's not like he's accusing me, exactly—in fact, I can tell he wants me to offer up an explanation he can believe. Still, he's not going to buy some trumped-up excuse that's obviously just that—an excuse. I don't blame him.

All at once I'm so exhausted by my lies. It feels like they're stones piled on top of me, a tremendous weight rendering me immobile. I long to fling them all off, send them flying in every direction. I could just blurt it out right now: Emilio, I'm a girl.

I open my mouth. Nothing comes out.

"If you don't like her, it's okay," he says, running a hand over his face.

"Who?"

"Erica! Come on, man, what's wrong with you?"

"She's nice. Really," I say weakly.

"So why are you feeding me this bullshit about your dead uncle?"

Our eyes meet and lock. The muscle in his jaw pulses.

"Emilio," I say in a low, steady voice, "there are certain things I can't tell you right now. I want to, but I can't."

"Like what?"

I groan in frustration. "You're right, okay? I don't have a dead uncle. Sorry if I hurt Erica's feelings. I don't want to hurt anyone."

"So don't then."

"It's not as simple as that."

"You totally ditched her. It was rude, man." His eyes blaze.

"I know, but you've got to trust me when I tell you I had no other choice. I'm not going to lie to you—"

"You already did."

I sigh. "I'm not going to lie to you again. I had to leave

right that second, and I had a good reason, but I can't tell you what it was."

He stalks around the room for a moment, clearly angry but trying not to be. His hands are shoved deep into his pockets. Finally, he stops at the foot of my bed, studies me, and says, "Okay. You had your reasons. Fine."

"Whatever happens, I want you to know I really like you. You're a great friend. Seriously. Okay? Will you keep that in mind?"

He sits on his bed, regarding me warily. After a long silence he says, "You okay?"

I collapse back into my pillow. "It's just been one of those days. I'll call Erica tomorrow and tell her I'm sorry."

"She's not doing too great right now, what with Julio and all that."

"Yeah. Shit. Sorry."

He doesn't respond; he just crawls under the covers. After a moment I do the same. We turn out the bedside light and stare at the ceiling, neither of us speaking. I think about how understanding he's being, despite my bizarre, erratic behavior. In contrast, I wonder what it'll take to patch things up with Chloe. I ask myself why everyone seems mad at me today. Then I think about all the ways I screwed things up in the last twenty-four hours, despite my best intentions, and that pretty much answers my question.

I'm just starting to fall into that state between waking and sleeping. The world behind my eyelids is slowly sucking me in, sparks dancing in abstract, pre-dream shapes like a moving Kandinsky. I'm yanked back to reality when a shrill beeping explodes on the bedside table. Assuming it's my cell phone, I reach for it instinctively. Instead of finding my phone, though, I feel warm flesh—aaagh! The light flicks on and I see Emilio's hand groping for his cell. He picks it up and studies the screen, rubbing his eyes.

"No way." He sits up in bed, his bare chest erupting out of the crisp white sheets.

"What is it?"

"Scheisse."

Oh, wow. He used my signature curse. I must be rubbing off on him a little. The idea fills my heart with molten happiness. I blink at him sleepily, unable to wipe the goofy grin off my face.

"What happened?" I ask.

"It's Summer."

That gets rid of the grin instantly.

"What a mess." He's texting, his face creased with concentration. "She's got an audition tomorrow in LA."

"But you guys open tomorrow." I sit up, hugging my knees.

"I know! And the audition's at four o'clock. There's no way she can get back in time."

"She can't do that! She doesn't even have an understudy, does she?"

He shakes his head, still texting. "Nope."

We're silent for a moment while he sends another missive. Almost instantly, he gets a reply. "She says her agent's making her go. It's for a huge movie and the role's perfect for her. She'd be playing Sarah Jessica Parker's daughter."

"But then you guys are totally screwed."

Another pause as several texts fly back and forth between them. Finally, he puts it back on the nightstand, shaking his head. "She's leaving first thing in the morning."

"That's horrible!"

"'Can't pass up the opportunity.'" The way he says it, I can tell he's quoting her.

"Still . . ."

"We'll have to cancel the opening." He looks dazed. "My mom was going to come up. She's got her tickets already— and only one night off work."

"Oh my God!" In my distress, my voice creeps up to a much girlier register. He shoots me a look. I force it back down. "Dude! That sucks."

Wheels inside my brain are turning. I know the role of Cecily. Of course I do! I know it so well it's practically encoded in my DNA. I'm not familiar with Mr. Pratt's blocking, but I'm usually pretty good at intuiting that stuff, and with a little coaching I could stumble through.

But wouldn't that be risky? Would costuming and makeup be enough to keep the guys from recognizing me? Maybe, maybe not. It would only be one night, though. And anyway, tomorrow's my last day at Underwood. The story's due Monday. Even if they recognize me, it will be too late to interfere; my research will be complete. I sneak a peek at Emilio, who is staring into space, a forlorn expression on his beautiful face.

I take a deep breath. "I might have an idea."

He turns his head toward me listlessly. "What?"

"Well, remember that cousin I mentioned?"

"Yeah . . ."

"She . . . um . . . she knows the role. Really well. She learned it as an understudy once."

"For real?"

I nod. "At Mountain View High. She still knows it, I bet."

"Yeah?" He considers. "She any good?"

"Hell yeah."

"No offense—I'm just asking."

"She's ten times better than Summer Sheers," I say, "that's for sure."

He thinks for a moment. "What's her name?"

I swallow. "Natalie Rowan."

"She was Summer's understudy, right?"

I nod.

"Summer mentioned her. Said she's pretty bad."

"Really?"

"Said she's kind of a prima donna too—hard to work with."

"Oh yeah?" I say through clenched teeth. "What else did she say?"

"Don't remember. I just got the idea they don't get along."

"Right."

"Why are you looking at me like that?" he asks.

"Like what?"

"Like you're about to tear my head off. I didn't say it, Summer did."

I take several deep breaths and force a smile. "Anyway, the point is, Natalie can do this role."

He sits up straighter. "You really think she would?"

"Tell you the truth, she doesn't like Summer much either. I think she'd enjoy the chance to prove what she can do."

"Awesome. Should I text Mr. Pratt? Oh, no, I guess you better check with her first, right?"

I nod. "Good idea."

I pick up my cell and call Darcy.

When she answers she says, "I'm working on Chloe, but she's still a little pissy."

"Hi *Natalie*," I say pointedly.

"What? Are you going crazy or something?"

"This is *Nat.*"

She says, "Oh, I get it. You're with someone?"

"Yeah, I'm here with Emilio, my roommate, and he tells me Summer Sheers just bailed on opening night for *The Importance of Being Earnest.*"

"No way!" she shrieks. "Is this for real?"

"That's right. So I told him my *cousin, Natalie,* can do the role of Cecily in her sleep."

"Oh my God! Seriously? You're going to do it? That's crazy!"

"But you'll probably need some help from your friends Darcy and Chloe with hair and makeup." I look over at Emilio, who wears a worried frown.

"Hair and makeup?" he whispers. "Why, is she disgusting? Summer said she's pretty manky."

I shoot him an annoyed look. "No, she's not 'manky.' Summer's just jealous."

"This is so exciting!" Darcy squeals. "Terrifying, but cool. What happened to Summer?"

"Audition in LA."

"Beeatch!" Darcy proclaims.

"Exactly. Anyway, *Natalie*, do you think you can get *Darcy and Chloe* to help out, or are they still pissed at you?"

"Hey, I was never pissed," she says, indignant. "And this'll be just the thing to snap Chloe out of it. You know she can't resist a makeover."

"Okay, great. Tomorrow, right after school, can you meet them in the girls' dressing room?"

"Right on," she says. "See you then."

I put the phone down and grin at Emilio.

"She'll do it?" he asks.

"Oh, yeah," I say. "She'll do it. You can text Mr. Pratt now if you want."

He picks up his phone and starts texting. After just a few seconds, though, he pauses to look at me appraisingly. "What's she like?"

My heart flutters wildly, but I try my best to exude confidence. "You're going to love her. Trust me."

●●●●●●●●●●●●●●●●●●●●●●●

Chapter Nineteen

●●●●●●●●●●●●●●●●●●●●●●●

"$\mathscr{O}$kay, look," Chloe says the next afternoon in the girls' dressing room. "I'm trying not to be mad."

"I appreciate that."

Her eyes widen. She's not prepared for this softer, kinder me. Historically, fights between Chloe and me tend to be rare but epic. We both have terrible tempers and colossal abilities to hold grudges. That usually leaves poor Darcy working overtime like a frenetic Switzerland, trying to help mend the rifts between us superpowers. It's a slightly dysfunctional triangle, but familiar.

Now, though, I'm tinkering with the ancient balance of our friendship by giving in right away. Her astonished expression tells me I've got the advantage of surprise, so I press that.

"I never should have messed with you and Josh." I squeeze her shoulder. "If you don't want to listen to my impressions of him, you shouldn't have to."

She looks suspicious. "You did more than share your *impressions.*"

"You're right. I totally interfered. That was wrong of me. I'm sorry."

Chloe cuts her eyes to Darcy, as if asking her to vouch for my sincerity.

Darcy beams at her and pats me on the back. "I think it's great she's admitting she screwed up. Especially since she was only trying to do the right thing, right Natalie?"

"It's true," I tell Chloe. "I thought I was helping, for real."

She just looks from Darcy to me for a long moment, mystified by this radical new approach. "Fine," she says at last. "Let's get to work. It's going to take a lot to make you into a convincing girl."

"Don't push it," I warn.

She tousles my hair. "Just kidding. Give me an hour; you'll be so gorgeous, you won't know what hit you."

If this was a movie, now would be the time to cue the montage. It would be a cross between the *Princess Diaries* makeover and the *Rocky* training sequence: me removing my stubble; Chloe applying these intricate, very realistic false eyelashes; Darcy altering Summer's costume to fit me; me hamming it up in a shiny black wig Chloe stole from Mountain View High's costume shop; the two of them frantically showing me the blocking. Underneath it all you'd hear a soundtrack with a driving, slightly manic beat by some hip girl singer, thus infusing the images with feel-good emotions as light and sweet as cotton candy.

Let me tell you, the montage is there because the reality is incredibly tedious. It takes hours of painstaking work and squishes it down into forty seconds of frothy fun. My afternoon has been hell. I've subjected myself to more primping, cramming, and correcting than anyone in the history of high school theater. It's an Oscar Wilde triathlon, requiring enormous patience and endurance. By the time we get to the actual performance, I'll be too exhausted to stand, let alone deliver lines.

Chloe and Darcy have gone to great lengths to ensure the boys will never recognize me as Nat. They've made me way girlier than Natalie ever was. I'm wearing a long wig a couple shades darker than my natural hair color. My makeup is flawlessly applied; my eyes look huge and doe-like, my cheeks a delicate pink, my complexion smooth and creamy as ivory, my lips full and lush. My costume is surprisingly flattering: high, stiff collar, a body-hugging waistline that makes the most of my limited curves, a snug little jacket, all of it in a pale violet that looks great with my dark hair and eyes. If I screw up every cue and get the blocking ass-backwards, at least I'll look good while I'm doing it.

Though the afternoon is grueling, I have to admit it feels fantastic being a girl again. Getting gorgeous via Chloe and Darcy's labor-intensive ministrations is kind of like going on a chocolate binge after weeks of subsisting on saltines. Cecily is an über-femme character, so every minute spent rehearsing that role means letting my softest, pinkest self come shining through. I let my voice climb soprano-high, let my laughter trill coquettishly. I flutter my lashes and indulge in coy, ladylike hand gestures. It's so unexpectedly liberating to exaggerate every womanly instinct rather than tamping them all down. I never really appreciated how great it is being a girl—how much more we can get away with. I feel unbound, expansive, free; who ever would have guessed that playing a Victorian debutante could be so weirdly therapeutic?

At five we're almost done with my eyelash touchup when Emilio sends me a text. I read it while Chloe continues to meticulously apply one little clump of lashes at a time—a much more difficult process than the Halloween costume variety, but (she assures me) infinitely more realistic.

Tried to find you but you've disappeared. Hate to ask, but can you take Erica to the play tonight and the party after? She's bummed about last night.

"Shit! I forgot to call Emilio's sister!"

"Move and I'll murder you," Chloe warns, staring at my eyelid with the concentration of a brain surgeon.

"How did that go, anyway?" Darcy's at my feet, hemming my dress.

"Total disaster."

"Really? Why?" She speaks with only half her mouth, since the other half is occupied with pins.

"Tell you later. Right now I have to deal with Emilio."

I type: *Can't take her to the play, but I can meet her at the party.*

Before I hit SEND, though, I ask, "Can you guys turn me back into Nat after the show, before the party?"

"Why?" Chloe wrinkles her nose. "Don't you want to go as a girl?"

"Emilio wants me to take his sister, which means good-bye Natalie, hello Nat."

"What? Like you do everything he says?"

I sigh. "I know. It's pathetic, but for some reason I can't say no to him. Can you fix me in time to get to the party?"

Darcy looks thoughtful. "I think it's a good idea, actually. In costume and with all this makeup, none of the guys will recognize you, but if you go to the party as Natalie they'll probably figure it out. We'll be fashionably late."

"Okay," Chloe breathes. "Man, the things I do for you."

I hit SEND. Darcy's right; it's too risky showing up at the party as myself. Going as Nat might allow me some form of good-bye with Emilio, however convoluted and awkward. My nose prickles the way it does before I start to cry. The thought of seeing Emilio for the last time makes me feel like I'm standing at the edge of a cliff, staring into the dizzy abyss below.

"Christ, you're not going to cry, are you?" Chloe asks in alarm. "You'll ruin your makeup, and then I'll have to kill you."

I swallow the lump in my throat. "No. I'm fine."

Darcy looks up at me, takes the pins from her mouth. "You really do like him, huh?"

Before I can answer, a text comes through from Emilio. I hit READ.

Thanks, man. You're the best.

It takes an iron will to hold the tears back, but I manage. Chloe's being quite literal when she promises to murder me if I shed even one.

Mr. Pratt paces the stage with glazed eyes, looking vaguely crazed and distinctly sleep-deprived. His bleached blond hair stands up at unnatural angles and his skin has an unhealthy sheen.

It's six o'clock; the show starts at eight. We're going to run through my scenes as quickly as possible, focusing on the blocking. I'm standing in the wings, having dashed to the bathroom for a quick pee—nerves reduce my bladder to the size of a lima bean. The other members of the cast are assembled onstage, waiting. Darcy and Chloe sit on the couch, Emilio stands by the fireplace stage right, Josh sits in a high-backed chair sneaking furtive glances at Chloe. Ms. Honaker, who plays Miss Prism, my governess, stands primly near Josh's chair. Max, Earl, and Tyler sit on the floor stage left. I know we've got very little time to get this right, but still I hesitate, terrified someone will recognize me. Nobody else is in costume yet, but I'm fully decked out; we're counting on the elaborate stage makeup, wig, and Victorian garb to make it impossible for anyone to realize I'm Nat.

Mr. Pratt looks at his watch. "As you all know, Summer got called away for an audition at the last possible moment."

"Ditched us," Josh mutters.

"Yes, well, be that as it may, we have very fortunately secured a replacement for her tonight, Natalie . . . ?" He looks at Darcy and Chloe.

"Rowan," Darcy supplies.

"Natalie Rowan, who knows the part well and will join us any second. Since I'm playing Reverend Chasuble I can't be on book, but Earl has generously offered to provide prompts from the booth in case anyone gets stuck."

I summon all my courage, stand tall, and make my entrance.

Mr. Pratt turns to me. For a fraction of a second, I think I detect a flicker of recognition in his bloodshot eyes, but then I see only relief.

"Here she is now! Natalie Rowan, our savior."

I walk to Mr. Pratt's side, keeping my eyes on him. Then I turn and survey the cast, heart racing. Ms. Honaker beams at me. Darcy winks. Chloe smirks. Josh lowers his chin and gives me a long, appreciative once-over. Earl and Tyler stare at me slack-jawed, while Max wears a tight little smile.

Finally, I let myself look at Emilio. He drinks me in with his dark, shining eyes. His expression is carefully guarded. It's like peering through a window in bright sunlight; I can sense movement, but the glare keeps it too opaque to reveal any details.

"Hey, everyone." I use my natural voice. "I know this isn't ideal, but I'll do my best to help out."

Mr. Pratt puts a hand on my shoulder. I swear there's a knowing sparkle in his eyes, and my breath catches. Oh, God, he's going to out me right here, right now. Once again, though, the expression gives way seamlessly to pure gratitude.

"Excellent." He removes his hand from my shoulder and rakes it through his disheveled hair. "We've got lots of work to do, folks. Let's get started."

Chapter Twenty

"*Y*ou're amazing." Darcy's gloved hand squeezes mine tightly just before I go onstage for the second time. "*So* much better than stupid old Summer Sheers."

"Is my makeup okay?"

She studies me a moment in the dimly lit wings. "Perfect."

This is my big proposal scene with Emilio's character, Algernon. So far, the show's run so smoothly it's almost scary. Just before I went on for the first time I thought my heart might explode, it was beating so recklessly; as soon as I felt the heat of the stage lights on my face and heard my voice saying my first line, though, I knew I could do it. It was like my whole body filled with helium. I became instantly buoyant, invincible. Every line popped right out of my mouth before my brain could get in the way.

"Knock 'em dead," Darcy says, giving me a little push.

I step out onstage, my heart rate accelerating once again. My stomach feels like it's inhabited by a litter of newborn kittens. Before I know it, though, I'm saying my lines, and Emilio's answering, and we're cutting through the dialogue like a sailboat slicing across the open water. The audience loves us; I can feel them hanging on our every word.

I know what's coming, though. It's like the roar of a waterfall getting louder and louder, pulling us toward it, drawing us in. The kiss. The one bit of blocking we didn't rehearse this afternoon.

"What a perfect angel you are, Cecily." Emilio kneels before me, his eyes searching my face.

"You dear romantic boy."

That's his cue. He stares at me, his face filled with both fear and wonder, like a child watching a lightning storm. I lick my lips. A trickle of perspiration slides down the back of my neck. Everything's in slow motion. My senses are so heightened, I can smell our makeup, our sweat, the waxy-clean scent of the recently mopped stage. Our bodies seem to be connected by an intricate net of electric impulses, crackling threads pulling tighter as our faces inch closer, our lips almost touching now. Finally, after what seems like hours but must be seconds, our mouths meet. His lips are unbelievably soft and warm. Behind my closed lids I see explosions: fireworks unfurl slowly against a tangerine sky. I lose all sense of the world beyond the crush of his mouth on mine, the melding of our tongues, the pressure of his hand on the back of my head, pulling me in to deepen the kiss.

I have no idea how long we linger there, getting drunk off each other. The moment hangs suspended, weightless. Then someone in the audience sneezes and my awareness snaps back to the stage. He seems to regain consciousness simultaneously and reluctantly we pull apart.

I'm dizzy. Opening my eyes, his expression reflects my own dreamy surprise.

As Mr. Pratt instructed, I run my fingers through his short, dark hair. "I hope your hair curls naturally, does it?" The line doesn't make a lot of sense, since his hair is way too short to curl, but the audience doesn't seem to mind.

"Yes, darling." His voice is husky. He clears his throat. "With a little help from others."

After the curtain call, backstage, everyone is cranked. We all hug and laugh and scream with such self-congratulatory jubilance you'd think we just launched a space shuttle or cured cancer or something.

Mr. Pratt wraps me in a bear hug so tight I can barely breathe. "You saved us, you brilliant girl!"

"Ah, it was nothing."

"Nothing? It was amazing! You didn't flub a single line. I have half a mind to drop little Blondezilla and put you in for the run of the show."

"Thanks," I say sincerely. "That means a lot to me. You're a great teacher, by the way."

He stops short. His eyebrow, several shades darker than his platinum hair, quirks sardonically. The chaotic hoots and spastic laughter of the cast and crew continues unabated all around us.

"A great teacher, huh?" he repeats slowly.

Scheisse! My hand nearly flies to my mouth when I realize my mistake, but I manage to halt the motion just in time.

"How would you know?" he asks, narrowing his eyes.

"Of course you're a great teacher—everyone says so. I'm sure it's true. And you taught me the blocking so easily. You're obviously really good at explaining things. I wish I could go to Underwood! I'd love to take your class," I babble.

"I bet you would." He nods, a mysterious smile tugging at the corners of his mouth.

Chloe and Darcy pounce on us then, their hats torn from their heads and their faces flushed with triumph. They engulf me in a fierce hug. Over their shoulders, though, I can see Mr. Pratt backing away, wearing a crafty, knowing expression that makes me nervous.

"You kicked ass!" Chloe says. "And man, those eyelashes still look awesome, even though you sweated like a sumo wrestler."

"Shut up," I laugh.

Darcy leans in closer and says in a conspiratorial tone, "That kiss in Act Two?! Holy shit. I thought you guys might set off the fire alarm!"

"No kidding." Chloe fans her face with her hands. "Mama mia, get a room!"

I squeal with delight in spite of myself. Remembering the fragile perfection of that moment obliterates any worries about Mr. Pratt or his suspicions. Somehow, hearing my friends say out loud what I know in my bones gives me hope. It's the best sort of validation. Emilio and I have chemistry. We have spine-tingling, toe-curling *je ne sais quoi*. Everyone in this whole theater felt it; does it get any more real than that? We became friends as guys, yes, but can't soul mates overcome even that? Doesn't a kiss that perfect deserve an encore?

"Don't look now," Darcy breathes, "Algernon incoming."

Of course I jerk around like a spaz and find myself nose to nose with Emilio. Heat spreads across my cheeks. Chloe and Darcy giggle and stumble away from us, holding each other up like a couple of drunks.

"Hey," Emilio says.

"Hey," I echo. Brilliant, Natalie. Such a scintillating conversationalist.

"Good work out there. You put the rest of us to shame."

I shake my head. "No! You were fantastic."

"I, um . . ." He looks at his shoes, looks up at me, looks at his shoes again. "I really loved working with you. It was so fun."

"Yeah. Me too." I tuck a strand of hair behind my ear. It's a total rush being a girl with him! I can't believe I'm finally allowed to flirt. At the same time, it feels so weird starting over as strangers when I already know him so well. I'm afraid if I open my mouth, something Nat knows but Natalie doesn't will fly out, incriminating me, like with Mr. Pratt.

Emilio shrugs. "Anyway, I just wanted to tell you what a great job you did."

"Thanks." I ransack the contents inside my head, searching for some way to prolong this conversation, but come up empty-handed. This could be my last chance to be a girl with him! Yet here I am, struck with a deeply inconvenient case of brain-freeze.

"You going to Josh's party?"

I frown. "Wish I could . . ."

"Oh, man! You've got to go. You're the guest of honor."

"I really can't."

"Why not?"

Because I've got a date with your sister.

"Previous obligations," I say vaguely.

It's both gratifying and heartbreaking to see how disappointed he looks. "Okay. Well, I guess I'll see you around. Thanks for saving the day."

Before I can think up a response he's turned and slipped into the crowd. I watch him go, feeling elated and crushed and confused all at once—a swirl of contradictory emotions so intense it takes my breath away.

Chloe and Darcy materialize once again at my side.

"He didn't recognize you, did he?" Darcy cranes her neck to catch a glimpse of him through the throng. Parents and friends from the audience have streamed into the green-room, adding to the chaos with flashing cameras, exuberant hugs, and cellophane-wrapped bouquets.

"No," I say, "nothing like that."

Chloe blows her hair out of her eyes, annoyed. "Well, what did he say?"

"Nothing much." I flash a brave smile, trying to shake the melancholy threatening to kill my post-show buzz. "Come on. Let's turn me into Nat one last time. After tonight, I'm going to be all girl all the time."

Getting back into Nat mode feels like putting on a sopping wet, too-tight pair of pants. Everything about it chafes and irritates.

Before Underwood I'd always assumed guys enjoyed more liberties than I did. They can get away with so much more, like walking alone late at night, sitting with their knees splayed wide, hocking up a loogie in public. So many of the issues girls agonize over don't seem to register with them—gaining five pounds or being called a slut or waking up with disastrous hair. I assumed being Nat would be a mini-vacation from all those worries and restrictions. I had vague notions that being a guy would mean stretching out in first class when I'm used to suffering through the cramped indignities of coach.

The reality? Going from being a girl to being a guy means amputating huge parts of myself. I've had to tamp down my instincts over and over again: Don't squeal, cry, or emote in any way; don't touch people or express interest in their welfare; do not, under any circumstances, be vulnerable. Of course, any time you're trying to act like someone you're not it's bound to be awkward, so I doubt being male feels this claustrophobic to actual guys. Knowing that does nothing to assuage my reluctance about jamming myself into the Nat Rodgers personae one last time.

"Are you sure you did the stoppelpaste right?" I sound peevish, even to myself, but I can't help it. "My jaw itches."

Chloe's makeup brush freezes in midair. She gives me a hard look. "I've spent all afternoon fixing your face, okay? I believe 'thank you God for saving my ass' is the correct response."

"Sorry. I'm just a little depressed."

Darcy is perched on the bathroom counter, flossing her teeth. "Depressed? That's crazy. You should be stoked."

"I guess." My voice is flat, listless.

"You did it, Natalie!" Darcy insists. "You did everything you set out to do and more."

I sigh. "What did I really accomplish? I have no real answers for my article. I'm not sure I understand guys any more than I did before all this. In the meantime, though, I've totally fallen for Emilio, who'll be pissed if he finds out I lied to him. And now Erica's involved—what will she say when she learns she's been crushing on a girl? What will Tyler, Max, and Earl think when they realize they've been had?" I fold my arms across my chest. "All I really did is tangle myself in lies. I'm hurting people I care about, for what? An article I probably won't even write."

Chloe puts her makeup brush down and fixes me with an inscrutable stare.

"What?" I challenge. "It's true."

She looks at the ceiling a moment, gathering her thoughts. "I'm only going to say this once, okay, so listen up. In the past week you've done more walking the walk than anyone I know. Yes, maybe this whole stunt's been crazy and misguided—so was doing this show with only a couple hours of rehearsal—but you tackled both, and you pulled it all off. Darcy and I look up to you, okay? You've totally proven just how bad-ass you can be."

Darcy jumps off the counter and hugs me. "She's right. You're amazing. We love you."

I start to cry. I can't help it. "Thanks, you guys."

"Now, can we stop stroking your ego and go to Josh's already?" Chloe looks at her watch. "Even the chips and salsa will be gone if we wait much longer."

I wipe my tears away and stand up. My gaze lands on Nat in the mirror. He's a part of me, I guess, just like every role I've ever played is a part of me. He's not a lie—not really. I still feel kind of sad and mixed up, but Chloe's right. We've got to get to Josh's. Erica's probably there already, and I can't risk disappointing her and Emilio both by standing her up.

I raise a fist. "Let's get this party started."

●●●●●●●●●●●●●●●●●●●●●●●●●
Chapter Twenty-one
●●●●●●●●●●●●●●●●●●●●●●●●●

Josh's party is huge and completely out of control. His parents own a massive house on Strawberry Point overlooking Richardson Bay. I've heard the sisters are both in college and the parents are vacationing in Venice, so the house is empty—well, empty aside from the hundred-plus intoxicated teenagers pouring in like a swarm of locusts.

As we walk into the living room, the bass beat is so loud it thrums inside my chest. There are kids dancing on the couches, on the chairs and ottomans and tabletops; a tall skinny guy I don't recognize dangles precariously from the spiral staircase. Bottles, plastic cups, cans, and mostly devoured hors d'oeuvres already sprawl across every surface. Man, I'd hate to be the one cleaning this place tomorrow. Then again, a house like this probably comes with an army of domestic servants ready to swoop in and restore it to its original luster before Josh has even finished his first cup of coffee.

Right away, I notice there are lots of people from Mountain View High here—too many for comfort. Someone could easily recognize me. I guess if I manage to finish this article and publish it, everyone who reads our school paper will know about Nat Rodgers. Still, I'm not prepared to be outed here in front of my Underwood posse. Maybe I should give up my Story of the Year aspirations and let Nat die a quick, anonymous death after tonight. That might soothe my guilt about lying to Emilio and everyone else at Underwood. I could wait a couple months, let my hair grow, then figure out a way to meet up with Emilio as Natalie. Would he recognize me as his old roommate if I wasn't in a wig and heavy makeup? Could I level with him if he did?

I resolve to work all of that out later. The immediate danger is being recognized here by someone in the Mountain View High cohort; that would limit my options severely. The scene is so chaotic and bacchanal I might escape notice, but I don't want to count on that. Darcy's wearing a hound's-tooth fedora, so I snatch that and put it on, pulling it down low so it practically covers my eyes.

"Hey!" Darcy complains. "What are you doing?"

"Too many Mountain View High kids." I lean close to her ear to be heard over the din. "Don't want to be recognized."

She looks miffed, but apparently sees the necessity.

Finger-fluffing her hot pink hair, she doesn't bother with a response. Chloe leads us through the drunken throngs into a spacious and slightly less crowded kitchen, where Josh is pouring tequila shots for a bevy of scantily clad girls, none of whom look familiar. One of them downs a shot and Josh places a slice of lime between her glossy lips. This might not be too incriminating, except that he does it with his teeth.

Darcy and I exchange a quick look before gauging Chloe's reaction. She spins on her heel and walks back out.

"Guess you called that," Darcy says in a low voice.

"I'm not going to tell her 'I told you so.'"

"Good thinking."

We catch up with Chloe in a room upstairs that might be someone's office. There are bookshelves on one wall and a desk in the corner. It's quieter than the living room. French doors lead to a high deck overlooking the bay. I spot Erica and Emilio outside, leaning against the railing. Just seeing them stirs up a dust storm of nerves inside me. They're the whole reason I'm here, though. Obviously I've got to go out there.

I look at Chloe. She's chewing on her lip and staring at the ceiling with intense concentration, as if the answers to all of life's burning questions are about to be answered up there.

"You okay?" I ask quietly.

She nods, but goes on looking at the ceiling. Her teeth bite down on her lip so hard that the skin there turns white.

I turn to Darcy, who gives me the *I'll handle this* look. I flash her a grateful half smile and indicate Emilio out on the porch. She nods in understanding. It's amazing how much information can pass between us without a single word.

Dismissed, though still a little worried about Chloe, I head outside onto the deck. I tell myself the Erica-Emilio situation is more pressing; besides, I'm the last person Chloe wants witnessing her distress, since she blatantly ignored my Josh-alarms. Outside, the air is cool on my face; there's a thin layer of fog hovering over the water, and the air smells like seaweed. Emilio spots me first, and then Erica follows his gaze, a radiant smile lighting up her face when she recognizes me. The smile throws me. After my rude escape last night, I should think she'd be scowling. It would be just my luck if ditching her added to my Nat personae an alluring air of mystery. What a tangled web I weave! Another sharp pang of guilt shoots through me, but I ignore it.

"What's going on, bro?" Emilio reaches out a hand.

"Nothing much." As our palms slide against each other briefly, I remember the kiss tonight onstage and how electric it was, how right it felt. I force myself to focus on Erica. "How are you?"

"I'm all right." She leans back against the railing, her expression slightly guarded. "You sure did disappear in a hurry last night."

"Yeah, I'm so sorry about that. I meant to call you."

"That's okay. Emilio told me about your condition."

I raise my eyebrows, glance at Emilio. "Did he really?"

She nods. "It's nothing to be ashamed of. A lot of people have irritable bowel syndrome. I'm taking a nutrition class online right now, and we learned all about it. You should alter your diet, though. Definitely cut out the coffee."

"Oh. Yeah. Good idea."

Emilio's fighting a smile. "Nat, looks like you could use a drink. What can I get you?"

"Something that won't exacerbate my condition," I say pointedly.

"Nothing alcoholic, carbonated, or caffeinated," Erica advises.

"Well then. I guess I'll have water."

"Erica? You ready for a refill?" he asks.

She looks at her red plastic cup, hands it to him. "I'll have another beer, I guess."

As Emilio makes his way across the porch and into the house, I watch him, filled with longing. I'm so going to miss him. God, this is hopeless. There's no way I'll get a chance to say good-bye—not tonight, not ever.

I turn my attention back to Erica. "Did you see the show?"

"Yeah, I went with my mom. She's in town for the night."

"Right, that's what Emilio said. Did you like it?"

She laughs. "Uh-huh. I couldn't believe how that girl stepped in at the last second. She was really good!"

I look at my shoes, hoping my face doesn't show how much this pleases me. "I heard about that. You thought she did okay?"

"She did great! Emilio said she's your cousin."

"Yep. Natalie."

She studies me intently for a moment. "You two kind of look alike."

"You think?"

"Except she's a lot prettier." She punches my arm lightly.

"Do you think, um, Emilio liked her?"

Erica's eyes light up. "We should fix them up!"

I pretend to consider this. "That's not a bad idea, actually."

"I don't really like that girl Summer."

"No," I shake my head. "She's stuck-up. Plus she has a boyfriend. He can do way better."

"The four of us should go out sometime." She flashes a quick, flirty grin.

"Mmm . . . that's an idea." *That's never going to happen.*

Without any warning, she tugs my hand, pulling me closer. I look around in alarm. Then I feel her fingers running up and down my arm. "I really like you, Nat."

"Uh, I like you too."

"You're so easy to talk to. I feel a connection with you . . ." When I don't say anything she adds, "You know what I mean?"

"Sure." *Think, Natalie, think! You have to stop this before it goes any further.* "Listen, it's only fair to tell you that I'm not really looking for a relationship. I mean, you're very sweet, and you deserve someone as cool as you . . ."

"But you're not that guy, right?" she asks, her tone suddenly bitter.

"No, I'm not." *In more ways than you can possibly imagine.* "But I'm sure he's out there."

Tears sparkle on her lashes as she searches my face. "You're not even going to give me a chance?"

God, how did this get so intense so quickly? Suddenly I understand the freak-and-flee instinct I've always found despicable in guys. I look into her eyes, willing her to understand, though of course the situation is so convoluted that's patently impossible. "Please, Erica, just—"

Suddenly she snakes her arms around my neck, pulls me to her, and kisses me. This isn't a gentle I-understand-and-we'll-always-be-friends peck on the cheek, either.

This is a look-out-sugar-'cause-I'm-going-to-rock-your-world kiss. I taste lipstick and beer and tongue and start to pull away in a panic, but she has her hands clamped to the back of my neck. She's surprisingly strong, and it's clear I'm not going anywhere until she's had her way with me.

After what seems like forever, I hear somebody clearing his throat. "Sorry to interrupt."

Erica lets go and we both jerk around to see Emilio smirking at us, carrying two plastic cups.

"You're not interrupting." I wipe my mouth as casually as I can.

"No, I definitely am." Emilio winks as he hands me my water and Erica her beer. "I'll leave you alone in a minute so you can pick up where you left off."

Ew! I now officially want to die.

Erica slaps his arm playfully. "Shut up!"

He grins. "You won't believe who just showed."

"Who?" I'm eager to change the subject.

Instead of answering, he turns and peers through the French doors. "She was right behind me. Stopped to talk with Darcy and Chloe for a second."

My stomach feels like it just stepped onto an elevator and plummeted thirty floors. It's okay, I tell myself. Summer's in LA. It can't possibly be her.

"Who?" I repeat, only this time through clenched teeth.

"I told her all about your cousin, what a great job she did. It's such a drag Natalie couldn't come to—"

"Who?" I practically scream.

He gives me an odd look. "Summer. She finished her audition and came back early. She didn't get the part, and she's pissed. First thing she did when she got here was down three shots of vodka. Better not ask about—"

"I've got to go." I pull the fedora lower and start for the French doors.

"Hold on!" He grabs my arm. "When I told her about your cousin she said she really wanted to meet you."

"Sorry. Can't."

Erica looks hurt. "Where are you going?"

I don't bother to respond. Enough with the lies already. It's better just to shut up and bolt. I look from Erica back to Emilio. I stare for a moment into his eyes, tortured by everything I can't say. Then I turn to go.

I force my way through the French doors and navigate the office, which has gotten more crowded. Someone's smoking a clove cigarette, and the cloying scent makes me cough. I push on, using my arms to part the crowd, shoving gently when needed, barely seeing where I'm going. All I know is, I can't let Summer spot me. She'll figure out what happened and tell everyone. God, why did I even come to this stupid party at all? I can't believe Erica kissed me!

My mind swirls like a snow globe given a good hard

shake. Half-formed thoughts carom off one another. I pick up speed, shoving people out of the way less gently now as my heart throbs in my ears. Partiers turn angry faces on me when I push them aside. One girl with scary, painted-on eyebrows and bright magenta lips barks, "Watch it, buddy!" A pink-faced guy with a unibrow shoves me back, and I barely manage to regain my balance before scuttling on.

I pause at the second-floor landing overlooking the vast, open living room and kitchen below. Leaning against the balcony to catch my breath, I scan the scene for Summer. Downstairs the party has reached fever pitch; the music's cranked and dancers writhe against each other like worms packed together in a jar. Just looking at them gives me a tight, claustrophobic feeling in my chest. Getting through there will be almost impossible; there must be a back door. Once I'm safely outside, I'll text Chloe and Darcy so we can get out of here.

"Nat!" I jerk around and see Emilio pushing his way toward me, with Erica right behind him. "Wait up!"

It kills me to ignore him, but I have no choice. Concentrate, Natalie. Just focus on getting to the stairs and finding an exit. Don't think, don't feel, just go.

I've got my head down and have only taken a couple steps when a terrifying sight stops me dead in my tracks. There, blocking my path, is a pair of pale brown knee-high Dolce & Gabbana boots.

Summer.

"So *this* is the notorious Nat." She's wearing a pale pink dress and a filmy scarf. Her upper lip curls with snide pleasure. "I knew you were up to something."

Behind her, Chloe and Darcy appear, panting slightly.

"We tried to stop her," Darcy mouths.

It's over. By now, Emilio and Erica have caught up too. Emilio's expression is still injured and perplexed, but he tries to smooth it over. "So you two met."

"Oh, we met all right." Summer's eyes sparkle. "In fact, we already know each other quite well, don't we, *Natalie*?"

"Natalie?" Emilio looks confused.

"Uh-huh. Natalie." A wicked smile spreads over Summer's face.

Emilio chuckles nervously. "No, that's his cousin, this is . . ." But he trails off when he sees my expression.

"I—this isn't how I wanted to—*scheisse!*" I'm so flustered, it's all I can spit out.

He takes a step back. "What's going on?"

Summer's obviously thrilled by the sight of me cringing like a cornered animal. She projects her voice so that even the people in the kitchen can hear. Stage hog. "Yeah, why don't you explain? I'm sure everyone would love to hear about your cross-dressing adventures."

A ripple of murmurs spreads through the gathering

254

crowd. Fine. This isn't what I had in mind, but if she's going to force my hand, so be it.

"Okay, yes." I take off the fedora. "I'm Natalie and Nat. Both. I mean, obviously I'm not Nat, but I pretended to be Nat so I could—"

"So you could what?" Summer interrupts. "Sneak into the guys' dorm and learn all their dirty secrets? Brag about it later?"

"No, I . . ." But I don't know how to finish. She's right, in a way. I wanted to prove I could pull it off, an acting challenge and undercover journalism feat all rolled into one. Now it feels like so much more than that; I owe it to the guys who befriended me to write something real about their lives, but in the beginning it was mostly about me proving myself as an actress and a writer, both of which were under attack. "Okay, at first, it was kind of like that, but then—"

"You know what?" Summer's face is rigid with a hostility she usually covers up with saccharine smiles. "You're pathetic. You're obsessed with one-upping me."

"What?" I'm honestly baffled by this.

"I'm in a play at Underwood, so what do you do? You couldn't just audition for the role like a normal person, compete with me fair and square—no, you had to cook up an elaborate cross-dressing stunt."

"Believe it or not," I say, "this isn't about you, Summer."

"Ha!" It's more a bark than a laugh. "I like Emilio, and he just *happens* to be your roommate? Coincidence? I doubt it. All you care about is moving in on my territory."

"He's not your territory!" I shoot a glance at Emilio, who watches us with a mixture of disbelief and revulsion.

"You must be so insecure." She takes a step toward me, leans in until I can smell the vodka on her breath. "I feel *sorry* for you. Hope you enjoyed your one night as Cecily. Because let's face it: You'll never be anything more than my understudy."

"Cat fight!" Someone in the crowd yells, which elicits a couple of hoots and giggles. I see Tyler, Max, and Earl push through the throng, curiosity and confusion showing plainly on their faces.

I'll admit, I desperately want to do damage to Summer's perfect little ingénue face right now. I'm not a violent person, but something about her sneering, glossy mouth makes me want slam my fist into it. I take a deep breath. This whole situation is humiliating enough; I don't need to compound that humiliation by diving on Summer and rolling around like a couple of ghetto chicks, clawing and scratching while onlookers film us with their camera phones so they can post it later on YouTube.

"Hold on a second." Fighting to keep my voice steady, I look Summer right in the eye. "I didn't go to Underwood because of you, okay? I had my own reasons."

"Oh yeah?" Her lips twist into an infuriating smirk. "Like what?"

"I wanted to know how guys really think." I glance at Emilio, then Tyler. "I wanted to walk in their shoes. I knew I'd never get real answers as a girl, so I became a guy."

Some bozo hollers, "Dude had a sex change?" More laughter.

Summer looks extremely pleased that my impassioned efforts to explain myself are just a big joke to this crowd. "She's so flat-chested, all she needed was a haircut."

Breathe, I tell myself. *Retract claws. Focus on what matters.*

I catch sight of Tyler shaking his head, looking baffled. Max wears a cryptic little grin, and Earl's mouth hangs open in obvious shock. I need to explain myself better—I can't have them thinking this was all some stupid prank. How can I, though, when my own motivations are so tangled inside my brain?

"I really wanted to get at the truth," I say. "But in the process, I told a lot of lies. I made really good friends at Underwood." I summon all my courage and face Emilio. "I hope they'll forgive me for lying to them. They showed me a side of myself I never even knew existed. I'm grateful for that, I really am."

Silence. Emilio and I stand there, eyes locked, and the rest of the world seems to disappear . . .

Thwack! Somebody lands an amazingly hard slap on my

cheek. I spin around, stunned, expecting to see Summer. Instead it's Erica, glaring at me with savage eyes. "You *puta*! I can't believe I *kissed* you!"

The whole room seems to gasp in unison.

Summer cackles. "Oh my God! So now you're a lesbian?"

"Hey, I'm sorry." Ignoring Summer, I cover my burning cheek with one hand; it hurts like hell. Girl's got some muscles. "It wasn't my idea."

Behind her, Emilio stares at me, stunned. "Nat . . . I . . . is this for real?"

"Which part, exactly?"

His face hardens. "You lied to me. To everyone."

"No—well, yeah, in a way, but—"

"You were laughing at us the whole time, weren't you?" He shakes his head.

I feel tears stinging at my eyes. "No! I thought it was the right thing to do."

"Next time, leave me out of your research." He turns and, taking Erica's hand, pushes back through the crowd away from me.

My vision blurs. Tears stream down my cheeks. Some remote part of me observes that at least I'm not wearing mascara. I look around at all the faces, but none of them are familiar—everything seems distorted and surreal now, like something from a Hieronymus Bosch painting.

"Come on." I feel a hand on my elbow, turn to see Darcy at my side. "Let's go. We'll take you home."

Summer lets out a mean-spirited giggle. "It's just so cute that you're exploring your masculine side, Natalie. Love the facial hair."

Chloe steps between us and snarls, "Yo, she-bitch, let's go!"

That shuts Summer up. She might be vindictive, but she's not about to risk a brawl with Chloe. Darcy holds my elbow protectively while Chloe clears a path with dirty looks and snarky comments.

As they're guiding me out the door, I turn one last time, searching the crowd for Emilio's face. No luck, though. He's disappeared.

I can't help wondering if I'll ever see him again.

Chapter Twenty-two

We drive to Underwood so I can pick up my things. Darcy and Chloe wait in the car. We figure I have a better chance of dashing in and out without incident if I go alone, since girls aren't supposed to be in the dorms without permission, especially after hours.

I stuff my few belongings into the duffel bag and am almost ready to leave when I hear footsteps out in the hall. I freeze, half longing for and half dreading the sight of Emilio loping through the door. There's a knock. My heart beats so frantically I can feel it in my throat.

"Yeah?" I croak.

The door opens a crack, and Tyler peeks around it, his expression uncertain. "Hey. You're still here."

"On my way out, though."

A look of hurt flickers in his eyes; immediately I regret my brusque tone.

"But I can stay a minute. What's up?"

He takes a step into the room. Behind him, I see Earl and Max. The three of them look almost scared of me, as if they've learned I'm a trained assassin and might pull a gun on them at the slightest provocation.

I gesture at the bed, where I've laid out Tyler's uniform with a Post-it note stuck to the blazer pocket. I didn't have time to write anything except *Please return to Tyler.* Now I feel ashamed of that hastily scribbled message. I owe these guys an explanation. They deserve that much.

"I, um, left your uniform. Thanks for the loan." I shove my hands into my pockets. After a week spent tamping down my natural exuberance, of curbing my urge to gabble on in a girly way, I suddenly feel more guy-like than ever. No words spring to my lips. All I can do is stare at the floor, embarrassed.

It's Max who breaks the silence. "I think what you did was amazing!"

I look at him, shocked. "You do?"

"It was brave and reckless, straight out of Shakespeare." His eyes shine with real admiration.

"At least you make more sense now," Tyler says. "All those weird questions you were always asking? We figured you were just socially retarded."

Earl nods, a half-ironic smile on his lips. "Which was something we could relate to, at least."

I giggle, then stop myself. For half a second silence threatens to settle over us again, but then we all burst out laughing at the same time.

"So you guys aren't mad?" I ask.

"Why would we be mad?" Tyler shrugs. "I mean, it's weird, but we're not exactly experts in 'normal.' Weird's okay."

"I tried getting answers as a girl," I explain, "but nobody would be real with me. It was the only way I could get the inside scoop."

I shut up abruptly when I hear more footsteps in the hall. Emilio? My heart speeds up again. Maybe he's come to apologize for what he said at the party. That's absurd—why would he? He was right—I totally lied to him. These guys aren't mad, though. Still, I never got as tight with them as I did with Emilio. I haven't betrayed them in the same way, somehow.

When the door swings open again, though, it's not Emilio who appears there but Darcy, her hound's-tooth fedora pulled down over her hot pink hair. Her eyes peek out from under the brim furtively.

"What are you doing?" She keeps her voice low, addressing me. "Your cover's blown—you've got to get out of here. We could get in trouble just for being on campus!"

I see the way Tyler's face lights up at the sight of her. He gazes at her like an eager puppy dog. I wish I could do something to help him make headway—something to bridge the gap between them. I really think they'd get along, if only they could get past the initial awkwardness. Darcy's right, though. We've got to go. Now's not the time for matchmaking or shooting the breeze with these guys. When Underwood administration learns of my deception, I'll be in major trouble. I've got to skedaddle, like pronto.

"Listen, I'll be in touch," I say to them.

They nod as I sling my duffel bag over my shoulder.

"Don't worry," Tyler assures me. "We won't nark."

"You guys are awesome." I hesitate, unsure of how to say good-bye. Then, on impulse, I throw my arms around Tyler. "Thanks for everything."

He turns beet red. "Yeah, no worries."

Since I've hugged Tyler, it feels weird not to do the same with Max and Earl. Max squeezes me tightly, uninhibited, but Earl angles his body slightly so that I end up awkwardly gripping his side. Whatever. It's the thought that counts.

"Tell Emilio . . ." But I don't know how to finish. "I'm sorry, I guess."

Tyler nods, his expression grave. "I'll tell him."

When we've passed the brass sign announcing Underwood Academy, Chloe heaves a sigh she's obviously been trying hard to suppress. "This was supposed to be a happy night. How did it turn into such a train wreck?"

Darcy glances at her in the rearview mirror. "Seriously."

"It was opening night! Natalie finally got to play Cecily, and she rocked the house. I was going to get it on with Josh, except he decided to molest those tweens. Who were those skanks, anyway? I feel like calling up their parents. 'It's midnight. Do you know who your offspring is blowing?'"

Darcy giggles, then tries not to, shooting a worried look in my direction. I'm riding shotgun, staring straight out the window in grim silence.

"Come on, Natters!" Chloe leans forward from the backseat. "Life sucks, but moping isn't going to fix anything, is it?"

I shrug.

"Will it make you happy if I admit you were totally right about Josh? He's a shit, and I should have listened to you. We know you love being right." She pokes me in the shoulder playfully.

I find myself fighting a smile. "I'm not going to say 'I told you so'—"

"Oops!" Chloe pokes me again. "I think you just did."

"Shut up!"

"I'm starving," Chloe complains. "What's open?"

That's how we end up spending two hours at Denny's chowing down on French fries and milkshakes while analyzing my undeniably fascinating week at Underwood. I feel like a soda can that's been shaken up—a whole week's worth of thoughts and feelings erupt in a foamy geyser of words. I move my hands as I talk, reveling in the freedom to gesture and shriek and giggle without restraint. I didn't realize just how repressed I'd been as Nat—how abbreviated. I bask in their rapt attention, giddy with relief and weak with gratitude for their *mm-hms* and *Oh my Gods*.

Around one a.m. I deflate abruptly. I remember Emilio's last words to me, the profound disappointment in his eyes, and it makes my chest ache.

"So now I guess Emilio hates me." I pick up one of the last stubby French fries and drag it listlessly through a smear of catsup. "I don't blame him, really."

"Why, though?" Chloe asks. "I don't get that. You had to lie to him or the whole plan would have been whacked."

"I betrayed his trust. That's a big deal for guys—especially someone like him who doesn't let people in that easily."

Darcy slurps the last dregs of her milkshake. "I can see that. He'll get over it though, won't he?"

"I doubt it." I slump back against the booth. "It's sad, because I really bonded with some of those guys—Emilio especially. In some weird way I was more myself with him than I've ever been with any guy before."

Chloe arches an eyebrow. "Forgive me, but weren't you pretending to have a penis? That hardly seems like the real Natalie Rowan."

"I couldn't manipulate him, though, you know?" I gaze at the ceiling, remembering. "I couldn't just giggle and flip my hair to get what I wanted. I had to find some part of myself that was deeper than that. More essential."

"Don't knock the hair flip." Chloe demonstrates, and Darcy laughs.

I ignore them. I'm trying to put words to something I can barely grasp, struggling to connect the dots. "I saw a side of him he'd never show to a girl either. Maybe that's why he's so pissed. It's like I tricked him into being himself."

"The feelings between you are real," Darcy says quietly. "He's got to see that."

"Yeah." I tip my head back all the way, hoping they won't notice the tears that threaten to spill over. Being an expressive girly girl again is one thing; turning into a sentimental crybaby quite another. "I hope so."

Sunday night I'm a wreck. I spent the entire weekend working on my article. Actually, I spent most of it pouting in front of my computer. I'd type a few words, delete them. Type a sentence, stare at it for a long time, groan. Delete. I'd check my vitals: MySpace, Facebook, e-mail, Twitter. Then I'd check my phone to make sure Emilio hadn't called. I'd scribble some notes by hand, pour myself more coffee, and start the entire process over again.

Finally, at three a.m. on Monday, I sit straight up in bed,

electrified. When I crawled under my duvet four hours ago, I'd accepted that my Story of the Year entry was never going to materialize. I simply couldn't force the tangle of thoughts and feelings into anything that resembled a paragraph. Now it comes to me. I rush to boot up my laptop and begin to type.

A Girl's Guide to Guys:
Their Top Seven Secrets Revealed
by
Dr. Aphrodite (aka Natalie Rowan)

Okay, I know what you're thinking: what the *?#! Natalie Rowan is Dr. Aphrodite? I've been seeking advice from a girl whose relationship resume could fit on a Post-it note? Yes, it's true. I am indeed Dr. A. And yes, before now, my firsthand knowledge of love was severely limited. That's why your fearless Doctor spent last week risking everything for top-secret undercover research. I, Natalie Rowan, enrolled at Underwood Academy as a dude named Nat Rodgers. I cut off my hair, strapped down my boobs, and stuck a sock in my BVDs. Why did I do this, you ask? So that you, dear reader, might benefit from my tireless quest to understand the most mysterious of animals: the human boy.

Below you'll find answers to your burning questions about the secret lives of guys—all the things you always wanted to know but were too afraid to ask. Even if you did ask, you probably didn't get straight answers. Believe me, I tried. That's why Natalie Rowan had to die for a week so Nat Rodgers could be born.

1) When you say you're going to call and you don't, what happened?

This requires a little anecdotal evidence, so bear with me. While disguised as Nat, I went on a date with a girl. Before you cue the girl-on-girl porn reel, remember: I went on said date with a sock packed rather awkwardly into my underwear. Despite being a girl for seventeen years, prior to this experience I'd never really considered what we girls act like on dates. Let me tell you, the reality was eye-opening.

The girl I went out with—let's call her Jennifer— was perfectly nice. She was sweet and smart with a dazzling smile. I'm sure if I met her under normal circumstances I'd rush to fix her up with my most eligible bachelor-friend.

Being on a date with her, though, threw me for a loop. It was clear she had great expectations I was supposed to fulfill, yet decoding those needs from moment to moment felt like a warped game of charades. She wanted me to be Man of Mystery and her sleepover BFF all at once. How could I help but disappoint her? Then I realized something: Jennifer's cryptic, high-maintenance behavior was eerily familiar. I myself had behaved exactly the same way on numerous dates; I'd just never stopped to consider what it might be like on the receiving end.

So what am I saying? That he didn't call because you're a moody head case? No, that's not my point. Sometimes, though, "I'll call you" is simply the fastest way to escape the withering power of a girl's disappointed glare and/or the tremendous weight of her misplaced expectations.

2) Why are you so different when your friends are around? Which one is the real you?

Let's face it: We've all got a bit of the chameleon in us. The version of you who hangs with her girlfriends Friday night probably isn't the exact same you dragging her butt into homeroom Monday morning, right? Just because you behave differently in those scenarios, it doesn't mean one is the real you and the other is fake. The situations simply highlight different aspects of your personality. Human beings are infinitely adaptable; I hate to break it to you, but guys are only human. They're different with their friends because they're multifaceted, complex beings, just like us.

As Nat I saw a distinctly different side of guys

than I'd have access to as Natalie, which was the whole point of this elaborate stunt—to get past the smokescreen of guy-girlness and hit the pay dirt of rock-bottom honesty. What I didn't anticipate was the discovery of an actual Nat Rodgers alive and well inside me. I felt like a guy at times. At first it took all my concentration just to camouflage, but for brief moments here and there, guyness felt almost natural. Am I going to ditch my stilettos and start popping steroids? Hardly. But the guys I came to admire and relate to at Underwood brought out a side of me I didn't know was there. If that's not proof of how elastic our true identities are, I don't know what is.

3) What do you really look for in a girl?

There are as many answers to this question as there are guys, I'm sure. It would be presumptuous and stupid of me to try answering for all boykind, especially since we've established that they're complex and versatile, contrary to popular belief. I will say, though, that most of the stuff we girls think is super-important to guys usually doesn't factor in all that much. They're not fixating on your zit or your freshly waxed eyebrows or the new skirt you're wearing. I'm not going to say they don't notice your body, because obviously they do. Trust me, though, you're way more worried about the five pounds you gained than they are.

Here's my advice: No matter what you think he's looking for, have the courage to be who you are. Watching my own best friends around guys made me realize that sometimes we hide our best selves and project this other, more contrived girly puppet version of ourselves because we think that's what boys want. Guys aren't stupid. They sense when we're trying too hard.

4) Is it true that guys think about sex every eight seconds, or is that just a myth?

Unfortunately, my week at Underwood didn't magically grant me access to every male brain I encountered. A little Internet research told me pretty quickly that the whole every-eight-seconds-thing has no scientific evidence to back it up, incidentally. How often guys think about sex, or whether it can even be measured, is still a mystery to both me and the world at large, apparently.

I will say that however often they may or may not think about sex, they don't talk about it all that much. If my girlfriends are any indication of the norm, we're way more graphic in describing what we've done and what we thought about it. As girls, we deal in secrets. Sharing juicy, confidential

271

details is part of how we bond. Guys get to know each other by hanging out; they're way more likely to play video games than to confess their secret desires.

5) What's the surest way to tell the difference between a guy who's being sincere and one who's just looking to score?

Let's talk about a guy I met at Underwood. For our purposes, he'll be known as Zorro—I know, weird, but humor me. So Zorro expresses interest in one of my friends—let's call her Zsa-Zsa. She'll appreciate that. Anyway, Zorro loves Zsa-Zsa, or so it seems. And Zorro, just so you know, is HOT. We're talking steaming, camera-ready sweetness. He's charming, funny, talented, athletic. As Natalie, I had to applaud Zsa-Zsa for finding such a prize.

And then I met him as Nat.

I know, I just got through establishing that it's perfectly okay to tap different sides of ourselves depending on the situation, but Zorro's an extreme example. In the presence of girls, Zorro's Mr. Sensitive. When the ladies leave the room, though, he's kind of a sleaze.

Can anyone blame Zsa-Zsa for crushing on him big-time? Can we scold her for not wanting to listen when I warned her about his slimy side? Can we even be sure which one is the "real" Zorro? No, no, and no. That said, even Zsa-Zsa would agree she's occasionally willing to fool herself when it comes to love. Like most of us. When we look into the eyes of the Zorros we meet, a tiny red flag usually pops up, and we know we're being fed a line. If the line is so delicious we can't resist nibbling, so be it, but the red flag is there. Who can we blame but ourselves if we ignore it?

6) What can make you lose interest in a girl over-night?

Look, girls aren't the only ones who experience mood swings, okay? We're also not the only ones capable of changing our minds. Any number of variables can factor in between last night's good-night kiss and this morning's cold shoulder. Are those factors directly related to you? Maybe, maybe not. The point is, feelings can change—and often do—abruptly. It's one of the riskiest aspects of falling for someone, especially during these tumultuous years when we're young and restless.

Yeah, it sucks. No, there's nothing you can do to prevent it. Here's the key, though: Don't let it destroy your confidence. If he's gone off you temporarily, nothing will make it permanent faster than rabid clinginess. You're the same person you were when he worshipped you, right? Keep that in mind, and if he's just not into you anymore, then buy yourself a cute pair of shoes and strut your fabulousness elsewhere.

7) If you won't talk about your feelings, how are we supposed to know what they are?

We've heard about Jennifer, Zorro, and Zsa-Zsa. Now it's time to introduce someone I'm going to call E. God, this part is scary. It makes my heart pound just writing that single initial.

I met E. at Underwood, and though I was dressed as a guy, the girl in me fell hard and fast the very first moment I saw him. He wasn't slick like Zorro, but I found him immediately fascinating.

If I'd gotten to know him as Natalie, I probably would have done the whole hyper-girly thing, jerking myself around like a marionette, trying hard to be everything and anything I imagined he might want. Instead I spent time with him as Nat, and so was forced to learn his language.

Guys do have a language, and it does express emotion with startling clarity and nuance. The idea that they don't express their feelings is as absurd as traveling to a foreign country and claiming the natives can't speak simply because you don't understand what they're saying. Guys may not use a lot of "I" statements; they may not cry or gasp or scream "Oh my God!" when something moves them. All the same, there's plenty going on in there; if you want to understand them, you have to be still for a moment and pay attention to the whole picture.

E., for example, shoves his hands in his pockets when he's frustrated. He blinks sleepily, like a lizard in the sun, when he's trying to figure you out. There's a tiny muscle in his jaw that pulses when he's tense. I could go on, but why should I hand over all the answers to his riddle? He's an intricate, mesmerizing puzzle; I only succeeded at putting the pieces together because for once in my life I observed. I stopped talking long enough to listen— really listen—not just to what's said, but also to everything that goes unspoken. Normally I'd be so caught up doing my girly dance that I'd never pick up on the subtle quirks that make E. so E.

I'm not saying it's wrong to want your boyfriend— or dad, brother, friend—to say things out loud. Sometimes we need complicated, oblique emotions distilled into words, because otherwise it's hard for us to believe they're real. There is a divide, though, between male and female worlds, and those worlds have different rules, different customs, different cultures. To ignore all that and expect him to be fluent in your language without ever really bothering to learn his is pompous and pigheaded. It's like the ugly American who barges into someone else's country and barks, "Why can't you people speak English?"

Before I went to Underwood, I was arrogant. I lived in my own world and didn't have the sensitivity or experience to understand that not everyone lived there with me. I measured guys' worth using superficial, unrealistic standards, and that blinded me to a lot of remarkable underdogs hiding in plain sight. It's crazy that it took a sock in my underwear to help me see all this, but I'm grateful for the insight anyway. If I hurt people along the way, I'm sorry. Really, truly, deeply sorry. My intent was never to manipulate or lie to anyone, though I suppose I accomplished both along the way.

In the end, Underwood taught me less about the secret lives of guys and more about my own secrets—the aspects of myself I couldn't see because I'd never stepped outside myself long enough to observe them. I hope I'm a better person because of it. I hope the people I hurt can see past the prank to the very real respect and affection I feel for them. If not, I may have to take my own advice, buy myself some cute shoes and march on. I hope that's not how it ends, though. I hope this boy-meets-girl-pretending-to-be-boy story has a happy ending, one with less bitter and more sweet.

Chapter Twenty-three

"*Pass* me that apricot body glitter, will you?" I say to Darcy. "Oh, and the tweezers—see, by your elbow?"

"Got it. Is this green face paint working?" she asks.

"Oh, totally. Very, very wicked."

"Damn it, where's my flatiron?" Chloe digs through the closet, careful not to mess up her freshly polished nails.

It's Halloween and the three of us are in Chloe's bathroom getting ready for her annual costume bash. Every year we dress up as a trio: Charlie's Angels; the Three Stooges; Powerpuff Girls; Snap, Crackle, and Pop. This year we've decided to go back to our roots and do the *Wizard of Oz* thing. Ever since we got cast in that play in the second grade, the characters have haunted us. This time, though, we're mixing it up and playing different roles. Darcy is going as the Wicked Witch, Chloe's Dorothy, and I'm Glinda. It's no good getting stuck in a rut, after all.

To be honest, Glinda never really did much for me in the past, but right now she's exactly what I need. Ever since my adventure as Nat, I've been obsessed with the color pink. Actually, I'm a sucker for just about anything über-femme these days: butterflies, ruffles, sparkly nail polish, vintage Madonna. If a guy wouldn't be caught dead anywhere near it, I can't get enough. The time I spent as Nat made me appreciate with renewed verve all the pleasures and privileges of girldome. I guess you don't really know what you have until you try beating it out of yourself for a week.

Six weeks have passed since Josh's party, and I've had some time to reflect on my adventures at Underwood. Though I might be making up for lost time indulging in the trappings of girlyness, I still have a bit of Nat inside me. It's weird; in some ways, the stuff I learned there makes me appreciate being a girl more than ever, but it also makes me pause before I do something hyper-girly out of instinct. When I catch myself feeling insecure about how I look, I think of Erica fixing her clip that night in the café—how she seemed to think everything about her had to be perfectly arranged before someone could possibly like her. When I find myself smiling out of nervous habit, I think of the guys at Underwood, and how they never put on fake grins just to please people. Sometimes I catch myself blabbering on about something giddily, and then I stop, remembering how relaxing it was sometimes at Underwood just to be terse and straightforward—to say something in two words instead of monologue-ing endlessly to fill the silence.

I'm not saying my week as Nat completely transformed me as a person. It's given me a lot to think about, though. Also, since I was grounded for three of the past six weeks, I've had plenty of time to contemplate these issues in my room all alone—when I wasn't slaving away on a week's worth of missed homework, that is.

Maybe I should back up.

First, let me just say, my article didn't win Story of the Year. It didn't even place. Some homeschooled fifteen-year-old girl wrote about a support group for Marin County war vets, and I have to admit the piece was pretty good. They ran it in the *Mill Valley Herald*. I wasn't crushed or anything—really. Sure, I was glad neither Chas nor Rachel won, but at that point I was so over the whole idea of proving something to them. The main thing I cared about was writing something honest about my experience, and I'm pretty sure I accomplished that. Well, I also cared about what the friends I made at Underwood thought about what I'd done. I've been in touch with Max, Tyler, and Earl via e-mail in the past few weeks, and I count them among my friends now. They totally took my gender-reversal in stride. That's one of the great things about fringe types: They aren't so attached

279

to everything being normal all the time. Of course, there's one Underwoodie I'm particularly concerned about, one I think about almost constantly, but the jury's still out on his opinion.

Though I didn't win Story of the Year, my exploits did eventually reach a wider audience. Word of my undercover escapade spread after my public outing at Josh's party. A *San Francisco Chronicle* reporter even interviewed me about my experience, expressing my story much better than I did in my own article, to be honest. Well, it's early days; at least I know there's room for improvement in my work. How sad would it be if I peaked as Dr. Aphrodite and spent the rest of my life looking back on high school as my moment in the sun? The answer to that question is "very sad." Artists who get discovered in their youth inevitably end up in rehab.

Though overall I have no regrets about Underwood, I did pay a price for my crazy stunt. At times it seemed like a hefty one. My mom wasn't too happy about the deception, for starters. She grounded me for three weeks, which is pretty harsh for her; the last time I got grounded I was thirteen and had shoplifted lip gloss at Macy's, so that gives you a sense of just how strict she is. For a little while it looked like Underwood was actually going to press charges, which freaked Mom out even more. Once the story in the *Chronicle* came out and the community started holding me up as some sort of innovative gender-bending young journalist, though, they backed off. Underwood's lawyer sent one threatening letter, but after that we never heard from them again.

As for *The Importance of Being Earnest*, Summer played Cecily for the rest of the run, though Chloe, Darcy, and Tyler all assured me she never came close to topping my performance on opening night. I've decided I am going to audition for *A Midsummer Night's Dream* in the spring. Summer was right, after all: I would make an amazing Titania. If she gets it, so what? I might make a better Puck, and that could be more fun anyway. I look Puckishly androgynous now, with my hair short. I'd probably be a kick-ass Puck, actually, now that I think of it. Who says I have to be the Fairy Queen?

I used to go on about how important it is to totally transform yourself from time to time. I still believe that, but now I've added a caveat: Play as many roles as you possibly can, but know who you are deep down. I'm a girl in my heart, but playing a guy helped me expand on and refine my understanding of what that means. I'm Dr. Aphrodite, a serious journalist, a budding actress, a giddy teenager—I'm all of these people, and I'm sure I'll be many more before I die. There is a core me-ness at the center of it all, though, a still, small voice that tells me what's true. That's what I concentrate on now. That's what I listen to when life gets crazy.

That brings us up to now: Halloween. I've served my sentence at home, caught up at school, and I'm ready to paaar-tay. I survey my freshly applied pale pink false eyelashes in the mirror. Not bad. I watch as Darcy and Chloe put the final touches on their own makeup. *God, I love being a girl*, I think. I love dressing up. I love debating the pros and cons of kitten heels. I love scarves and potpourri and ordering drinks at Starbucks that are so complicated they require the baristas to use crib notes. Being a girl, I decide, is the bomb ticking.

"Oh, no," Chloe says, looking at me in alarm. "Are you getting all teary again?"

"I'm fine," I sniff.

She studies me, her flatiron suspended near her face. "What's up with you? Ever since Underwood, you've been such a sappy freak! Every time we get dressed up you get all weepy."

I fan my face, trying to hold back the tears. "It's just so beautiful."

"What is, exactly?" Darcy removes a strand of wig hair that's sticking to my glossed lips.

"Being girls! Don't you think? Isn't it the best?"

They exchange a private look.

"Whatever," I say impatiently. "You don't get it. I realize that. Believe me, though, if you spent a week with your boobs smashed flat waking up every morning to ten guys peeing at urinals, you would appreciate this moment."

"Uh-huh." Chloe looks doubtful.

"I'm serious!" I wail. "You would!"

Suddenly the doorbell rings. Chloe's eyes go wide and she slams the flatiron down. "First guests. I wonder who it is?"

Darcy stands up. "You ready, Freaks of Oz?"

I grin. "Let's do this!"

This year our annual Halloween bash is bigger and better than ever. By eleven, the place is packed with creatures of every ilk: werewolves and fairies, zombies and movie stars. As usual, a fair number of the guys have opted for minimal (think football jersey and blackened eyes), while lots of girls have gone with your usual "just add hoochie" philosophy (oh, look, it's the slutty nurse! And there's her friend, the slutty cowgirl). I look around the living room as Darcy leads a disorderly mob in a nutty dance routine she's worked out to her theme song, "Super Freak." Nobody's really keeping up, but they all seem to be having fun. When the song ends, I see a triumphant Darcy, glazed with sweat and laughing, fall into the arms of Tyler, who's dressed as Sonic the Hedgehog. Somehow, in the last few weeks, they've started seeing each other. He looks super-cute and deliriously happy. I watch with satisfaction as Darcy kisses him. She isn't quite ready to admit they're an actual couple (he is, after all, still a POKSI) but it's pretty obvious they're headed in that direction.

I wander into the kitchen, feeling a little forlorn. I sent Emilio a letter a week ago, but he hasn't responded. I almost e-mailed several times before that, but always ended up deleting my efforts. The screen seemed too cold, too clinical to convey everything I needed to tell him. Of course, paper didn't make it much easier. I went through ten drafts before I finally settled on one I could send. The final version ended up being one sentence: *I miss you*, followed by the necessary information about Chloe's party. Considering it's almost midnight and there's still no sign of him, I'm beginning to give up hope.

"Hello, Natalie." My heart skips a beat at the sound of a deep baritone voice saying my name. When I turn, though, it's just Chas Marshal standing there, eyeing me appreciatively. "You look great."

"Oh, hi Chas. Where's your costume?"

He purses his lips. "I don't really get into Halloween. You know me."

Yeah, I do know you: *boring!*

"By the way, I've been meaning to tell you, your column is better than ever these days," he says. "Your little stint at Underwood added some real depth to your writing."

"Thanks." I'm so floored by this uncharacteristic praise, it's all I can think of to say.

"Of course, you still need to work on your semicolons. They're superfluous eighty percent of the time."

There we go. That's more like the Chas I know and despise.

Rachel Webb appears at his side in a cream twinset, a tweed skirt, and pearls. She dabs at her nose with a Kleenex, ignoring me. "Chas, honey, I need to go. I don't feel well."

"Okay, sweetums. I'll get your coat."

Sweetums? Ick! Yes, my editors from Planet Suck have decided to combine their suckyness for an unholy union.

Watching them walk away, I can feel my mood sinking a couple inches lower. Apparently, even neurotic, punctuation-obsessed tyrants have more luck finding love than I do.

"Hey, Glinda! What you got up your wand?" Tyler punches me in the arm playfully. Beside him, Max surveys the room imperiously in a detailed Louis XIV costume.

"Necessary Good Witch supplies. You need some fairy dust?"

Earl comes running up to us in a furry black suit with a plastic feline mask. He makes a growling sound and flashes his claws at me.

"Nice work," I say. "You're a panther, right?"

He pushes his mask up onto his forehead. "The Black Panther, to be precise, also known as T'Challa. He made his debut in *Fantastic Four* issue number fifty-two, published in—"

"Okay," Tyler interrupts. "We get the picture. No need for the dissertation."

"Don't look now." Max adjusts his wig and purses his lips primly. "But Marilyn Monroe just walked in. Puh-leaze! As if she's got the hips to pull *that* off."

We watch Summer stride across the room wearing a white Marilyn Monroe dress, strappy sandals, and a platinum blond wig. She's arm in arm with Robbie, her boyfriend, who's settled for streaking his face in blood—how original. I wait for the familiar jealousy to tug at my guts, but it doesn't happen. Somehow, playing Cecily seems to have exorcised that particular demon from my psyche. I'm just not threatened by her anymore. I feel blissfully detached as I watch her work the room.

"How much you want to bet she pulls the old 'whoops, there goes my dress move' by the heater?" Tyler mutters.

"Oh, she's spotted it." Max nods. "Yep, she's moving in for the kill."

We all watch as Summer positions herself over the floor vent and squeals delightedly, holding her skirt down as it billows around her.

Tyler grins, shaking his head. "So predictable."

I laugh. "I miss you guys!"

"Glinda the Good Witch, huh?" says someone behind me. "Cast any spells lately?"

I spin around and there's Emilio, alarmingly close, his eyes the exact shade of espresso brown I remember. I open my mouth, getting ready to say something, but nothing comes out. Apparently my vocal cords have seized up.

Emilio smiles, noting my paralysis, clearly enjoying it.

"You made it!" Tyler slaps Emilio on the shoulder. "Good to see you, man."

"Hey Emilio," Max says, "happy Halloween. What are you supposed to be?"

Emilio looks down at himself. He has on ragged black pants shredded mid-calf, a ripped-up silk shirt, bare feet, and an eye patch. "Shipwrecked pirate," he says. "It was the best I could do at the last minute."

"Interesting choice." Earl nods in approval. "Pirates have a fascinating history. Did you know that during the golden age of piracy the colonial powers made it legal for English privateers to attack and rob Spanish ships?"

"Come on, guys." Tyler flashes me a knowing look, then grabs Earl with one hand and Max with the other, dragging them toward the living room. "Let them be."

Just like that we're alone—well, we're standing in a kitchen packed with creatures of every sort, most of them hunched around a rowdy game of quarters—but as far as I'm concerned, we're the only ones in the room.

"Don't look so shocked," he says after an awkward pause. "You did invite me, right?"

I clear my throat, hoping to jump-start my speaking apparatus. No luck. Here I've been telling him things in my head for weeks, writing long, frenzied missives to him I know I'll never send, and now that I have him less than two feet away I'm struck dumb. Fantastic.

"Oh my God, Grant Bryers just kissed me!" It's Chloe, out of breath and pink cheeked, moving as quickly as she can in her high-heeled ruby slippers. "Holy shit, he's so cute!"

I clear my throat again forcefully, as if trying to dislodge something—gross, I know, but this is apparently the only communication I'm capable of.

She looks from me to Emilio and back to me again. "He showed up!" When my only response is a scorching blush, she says to him, "Are you here to put her out of her misery?"

I have reason to believe Chloe's had a few too many of her specialty cocktail, the Trick-or-tini. Apparently, they've loosened her tongue in unfortunate ways.

"Well, I'm here, anyway." He looks amused.

Finally, out of sheer desperation, I find my voice. "You'll have to excuse her—she gets carried away."

Chloe reaches out and pumps his hand energetically. "Congratulations, Emilio. You're the only guy who's ever turned our Natalie into a basket case for more than a week. She won't shut up about you, I mean—"

"Catch up with you in a minute," I tell her, stepping between them slightly and bugging my eyes at her. "Okay?"

She just smirks and saunters off, shrieking something at Grant Bryers as she goes. I turn back to Emilio. "Sorry, it's—you know, Halloween. Everyone's all excited."

"Yeah." He glances at Zoë Showalter, who's tearing open her Velcro-fastened evening gown to reveal a pink sequined bikini beneath. "I can see that. Wow. You don't see that every day at Underwood."

I laugh. "I can imagine!"

"You're one of the few girls who really *can* imagine."

We look at each other for a long moment and the drunken shrieks, the pounding bass, and the sequined bikinis fade into something soft and remote, like the hum of a distant airplane. His eyes seem to be asking me something, but I don't know what, exactly, and before I've decided what to say in answer to the question I can't decipher, I open my mouth.

"Listen, Emilio, I know you were probably mad—maybe you still are—but I never meant to hurt anyone, it was just an idea for a story, and then I met you and it became . . ." I trail off.

He tilts his head quizzically. "Became what?"

"It became so much more. I mean, I became . . ." *His mouth*! I've forgotten just how full and perfect it is. ". . . emotionally invested." I blush again, look down at my shoes. "Bad idea, I guess."

"I read your article."

"You did?" I can't breathe as I try to decipher his expression. "And . . . ?"

"It was enlightening. Dr. Aphrodite? How many aliases do you have, anyway?"

Relief makes me laugh out loud. "Two, I guess, and counting . . ."

He runs one finger lightly down my arm, and I close my eyes, savoring the warmth of his touch. When I open them again I see he's taking me in, letting his gaze wander slowly down every inch of my body. For a second I'm embarrassed, but then suddenly I'm glad—so glad—he can see me in all my girly glory at last.

"Are you mad?" I ask.

"I was." He glances at the ceiling, then back at me. "Or confused, anyway. The whole thing threw me for a loop. I thought I'd finally met a guy at Underwood I could relate to, and it turns he wasn't a guy at all."

I swallow. "I can see how that would be weird."

"In a way, though, I was relieved."

"Relieved?" I echo. "Why?"

He looks around, embarrassed. "Let's just say you had me questioning my sexual orientation."

I laugh, then slap my hand over my mouth, trying not to be insensitive. It's just such a relief to know he felt the electricity that was driving me insane! "I'm sorry—how rude of me to make fun."

"No"—he grins a little sheepishly—"go on, have a good laugh. I'm sure it's hilarious."

"Emilio, really! I didn't mean to—"

But I don't get to finish my sentence. Suddenly he bends his head and kisses me, his full, perfect lips finding mine without hesitation.

I have to say it's the most sizzling, delicious, sublime kiss ever. In the history of human beings. Possibly back to and including dinosaurs.

"Huh," I mutter, when at last we pull away, both of us reluctantly. "And to think we wasted all that time as room-mates just *talking*."

"Don't worry." He touches my cheek gently. "I'll make it up to you."

I hear shrieks of delight coming from the living room. "Spooky Little Girl Like You," the Zombies song Chloe, Darcy, and I traditionally blast at midnight on Halloween, starts playing super-loud on the stereo. I can make out their voices calling my name at top volume—chanting it with the crazed enthusiasm only best friends can muster.

He smiles broadly. "Apparently you're being paged."

I giggle. It feels so good to be a girl around him—absolutely divine. At the same time, I know it was the five days I spent with him as Nat Rodgers that allows me to really understand him.

"You feel like dancing?" I ask.

"Uh . . . sure."

"Don't worry." I gesture at my petal pink stilettos. "I promise not to step on your toes."

"I'm not worried."

"Emilio?"

"Yes, Nat—alie?" He adds the last two syllables after the tiniest hesitation, which makes me smile.

"I'm really glad you showed up."

He throws back his head and laughs, then slips his hand across the small of my back and guides me out of the kitchen. "Believe me, spooky girl, there's no place I'd rather be."